"Tori, I want you to meet someone special."

Claudia gestured to Jake. "This is Jacob Holland, the eldest son of my dearest friends. Jake, this is my niece, Victoria Lerner."

Lerner? Of course. Did he really expect anything different?

The whisper of a memory filtered through his mind, but he forced it back into the dark corner where it belonged. Remembering equaled pain, and he'd had enough heartache to last a lifetime.

"Victoria." Her name slipped past his lips in a mix of a whisper and a gasp.

Victoria's clover-green eyes tangled with his. She wore a pink sundress that complemented her pale skin. She lifted her hand. "H-hi, Jake."

So maybe she wasn't as confident as she appeared.

Good.

He didn't need to be the only one feeling like he'd been kicked in the gut.

She smiled, creasing the dimples in her cheeks that could charm an ornery bull.

But not him.

Not anymore. He was immune. Had to be. It was his only protection against the devastation she was capable of causing.

Lisa Jordan has been writing for over a decade, taking a hiatus to earn her degree in early childhood education. By day, she operates an in-home family childcare business. By night, she writes contemporary Christian romances. Being a wife to her real-life hero and mother to two young-adult men overflows her cup of blessings. In her spare time, she loves reading, knitting and hanging out with family and friends. Learn more about her at lisajordanbooks.com.

Books by Lisa Jordan

Love Inspired

Lakeside Reunion
Lakeside Family
Lakeside Sweethearts
Lakeside Redemption
Lakeside Romance
Season of Hope

Visit the Author Profile page at Harlequin.com.

Season of Hope

Lisa Jordan

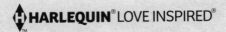

HARLEQUIN® LOVE INSPIRED®

Recycling programs
for this product may
not exist in your area.

LOVE INSPIRED BOOKS

ISBN-13: 978-1-335-47906-8

Season of Hope

www.Harlequin.com

Printed in U.S.A.

Come unto me, all ye that labor
and are heavy laden, and I will give you rest.
Take my yoke upon you, and learn of me;
for I am meek and lowly in heart: and ye shall
find rest unto your souls. For my yoke is easy,
and my burden is light.
—*Matthew* 11:28–30

In memory of my grandparents, Charles and Lillian Camp, whose planted seeds of authentic faith created a spiritual legacy that has been passed down to future generations.

Acknowledgments

Thank you to those who brainstormed, answered research questions and prayed me through the completion of this book:
Susan May Warren, Rachel Hauck,
Beth Vogt, Melissa Tagg, Alena Tauriainen,
Jeanne Takenaka, Michelle Lim,
Richard and Mindy Obenhaus, Tari Faris,
Tracy Jones, Kariss Lynch, Andrea Nell,
Michelle Aleckson, Tara Sleeman, Josh and Valerie White and my WWC church family.

Thank you to my fairy-godmother agent, Rachelle Gardner, and my awesome editor, Melissa Endlich, for your continued support and guidance as I grow as a writer.
Thank you to the Love Inspired team for your role in making this book happen.

Thanks to my husband, Patrick, and our sons, Scott and Mitchell, for your continued support and being my best cheerleaders.
I love you always and forever.

Thank you, most of all, to my Heavenly Father for allowing me to live my dream and always giving me rest for my soul.
Without You, none of this would be possible.

Chapter One

Jake hated betrayal.

Six years in the military fighting against injustice, terrorism and the oppression of the weak prepared him for great battles. But he didn't expect to be fighting one in his own backyard. For something that had been promised to him, to his family. By one of his own.

But Claudia wouldn't do that.

Would she?

No way.

She wouldn't be the first person to break her word…

Still, there had to be a good reason. It wasn't like her to go back on a promise, especially to family.

Well, he might not be family by blood, but Claudia Gaines had been his mother's best friend since college. And like a second mother since tragedy stole his five years ago in a freak accident.

Jake sucked down a breath, just enough for his heart-beat to slow in his ears, and rapped weather-beaten knuckles against the red-painted door.

Midmorning June breezes stirred Claudia's collection of colorful wind chimes, creating a symphony of low-toned woods clamoring with high-pitched metal. Just enough sound to rouse memories of the scorching desert sun, the air veiled with smoke and sand, the look of hopelessness in the faces of people trapped by a tyrannical government, and the night his life changed forever.

The night of ultimate betrayal that set him on a journey to bring hope to those courageous soldiers clawing for a way out—an escape from their private wars that raged long after returning home.

A journey that hit too close to home.

No wonder he'd taken to stretching out on his back deck and listening to the crickets and cows. Where the stillness served as a balm to the echoes in his head he couldn't seem to deafen.

Nestled between a national forest and a man-made lake, the lakefront community of Shelby Lake in northwestern Pennsylvania was a far cry from the Middle East. He preferred hanging out on his family's dairy farm spanning across most of Holland Hill on the edge of town.

His place of security.

Although he disliked coming into town on a regular basis, for once, though, he was thankful for Gossiping Gwen at the feed store. Otherwise, he might not have learned about the sale until it was too late.

He needed that land. He had a promise to keep. To atone for sins of his past.

But without Claudia's land, those promises would remain unfulfilled, and that was a risk he just couldn't take.

What was taking her so long to answer the door?

Cupping his hands around his eyes, Jake peered

through the slit in the curtains hanging on the other side of the glass, but he couldn't see much. His barn boots clomping against the painted gray planks, Jake crossed the wide covered porch, ducked his head under one of the hanging red geraniums and peered around the side of the house to see if her car was parked in the garage.

Not only was her cherry-red SUV parked in the driveway, but also a champagne-colored Lexus sat behind it.

Claudia had company.

At least he knew she was home.

He flung a leg over the railing and jumped down, missing the hot pink peonies blossoming in the side flower bed. Gravel crunched beneath his feet as he strode to the back porch, where the storm door stood open. Childish giggles streamed through the screen followed by barking.

Claudia didn't have a dog...

Jake opened the door and stepped into the pristine mudroom that smelled of fabric softener. Toeing off his boots, Jake called, "Claudia?"

"Jake? That you?" She appeared in the doorway to the kitchen, wearing a sleeveless blue dress and leather sandals. She dropped the dish towel she'd been holding into a basket on the washing machine and opened her arms for a hug.

Jake walked into her embrace, breathing in scents of vanilla and baked bread, and allowed himself to relax. For half a second, he'd worried something had happened to her, and he couldn't bear losing her, too. His family had suffered too much loss over the past five years. Claudia had been the glue that held them all together.

"I knocked on the front door, but you didn't answer."

"Knock? Since when does family need an invitation?" She released him, then grabbed his hand and pulled him toward the kitchen. "Come in and grab some coffee. There's someone I'd like you to meet."

Jake removed his sunglasses and hooked them on the edge of his gray T-shirt. He pulled off his tattered Ohio State ball cap, stuffed it in the back pocket of his jeans and finger-combed his hair quickly as he followed Claudia.

A childish squeal followed by giggles and more barking sounded overhead as footsteps thundered across the ceiling. He squinted gritty eyes against the bright sunshine pouring through the open kitchen window, over the sink and onto the ceramic floor tile. "I can't stay for coffee. I just need to talk to you for a minute."

"Sure, honey, but conversation is always better over coffee." She poured coffee into three red stoneware mugs and handed one to him.

With one hand gripping the back of the wooden kitchen chair, he sipped the dark roast she favored. The first sip went down smooth, warming his stomach. He released a sigh, feeling a little more relaxed since Gwen had shared her news. Claudia would assure him all was well and she intended to make good on her promise.

He'd stressed out for nothing.

Needing the caffeine jolt to his weary system, Jake gulped a mouthful of coffee, caught a movement out the corner of his eye and turned.

He stiffened.

Jake choked, shooting the bitter brew out his nose and across the white tablecloth. His eyes watered, and his chest burned as his lungs seized. Still coughing, he scrubbed a hand across his tired face.

Claudia pounded him on the back and handed him a towel.

He wiped his eyes and tried to scrub the coffee off the front of his T-shirt, but it was no use.

Heat scalded his neck and crawled across his cheeks. Bracing both hands against the back of the chair, Jake closed his eyes and forced air into his lungs.

A moment later, he dared a glance and wished he could turn back time to thirty minutes ago when he debated between calling Claudia or stopping by. If he'd known, he wouldn't have stepped foot on the property.

What was *she* doing here?

And *today* of all days?

Struggling for composure he didn't feel, Jake straightened all six feet two inches of himself and stood with his shoulders back, chest high, feet apart and hands clasped in front of him.

Claudia crossed the room and linked her arm with the wide-eyed woman frozen in the archway between the kitchen and living room. In her arms, she held a small child with blond hair who tucked her face in the woman's neck. A Yorkie with a black-and-tan coat wearing a pink collar sprinted over to Jake, sniffed his feet and then put her paws on Jake's leg.

"Tori, darling, I want you to meet someone special." Dragging the woman over to the table, she gestured to Jake. "This is Jacob Holland, the oldest son of my dearest friends. Jake, this is my niece Victoria Lerner and my great-niece, Annabeth. She belongs to Tori's sister, Kendra, who is currently deployed overseas. And that troublemaker begging to be picked up is Poppy."

Lerner? Of course. Did he really expect anything different?

The whisper of a memory filtered through his mind, but he forced it back into the dark corner where it belonged. Remembering equaled pain, and he'd had enough heartache to last a lifetime.

"Victoria." Her name slipped passed his lips in a mix of a whisper and a gasp. He swallowed and reached down to scoop up the furry animal begging for attention.

Victoria's clover-green eyes tangled with his. She set down the child, who gave Jake a shy glance before running into the other room.

Poppy wiggled in Jake's arms, and he set the dog on the floor so she could chase after the little girl.

Victoria's manicured fingers smoothed the top of her sleek head and toyed with the ends of her caramel-colored braid resting in front of her left shoulder like one of his niece's Disney princess dolls. She wore a pink sundress that complemented her creamy skin and white strappy high heels. She crossed one foot over the other and lifted her hand. "H-hi, Jake."

So maybe she wasn't as confident as she appeared.

Good.

He didn't need to be the only one feeling like he'd been kicked in the gut.

She smiled, creasing the dimples in her cheeks that could charm an ornery bull.

But not him.

Not anymore. He was immune. Had to be. His only protection against the devastation she was capable of causing.

With hands laced tightly in front of her, Tori looked at him with the soulful eyes that cinched his insides.

Give me strength.

He stuffed a hand in the front pocket of his faded, muddy Levi's and dragged the other through his hair that was about two weeks past needing a trim. He spiked a finger on a stray piece of hay. Feeling the effects of being awake since 4:00 a.m., Jake forced out a breath.

Claudia watched them with puckered brows and narrowed eyes. "What's going on? You two know each other?"

Jake shot a look at Tori, who dropped her gaze to the floor, then looked at her aunt. "We met years ago when I worked at the NCO club on base where Kendra—" she waved a hand toward Jake "—and Jake had been stationed. I spilled a tray of drinks on him and he was a perfect gentleman about it, helping me to keep my job."

That's it? That's all she was going to say? What about—

Claudia swatted his chest. "You never mentioned you'd met my beautiful niece."

"I didn't know she was related to you until now."

"Small world, huh?"

And getting smaller by the second…

"Something like that." He turned to Tori. "So, Victoria, what brings you to Shelby Lake?"

Before she could reply, Claudia pulled out a chair and tugged on Jake's arm. "Jake, have a seat. I need to talk to you."

"Me, too, but I'd prefer to do it privately."

"Okay, but hear me out first. Since it involves Tori, too, I'd like her to stay." Instead of sitting, Claudia opened a bottom cabinet near the stove and pulled out a small frying pan. She grabbed a carton of eggs from the fridge and set them on the counter. "Want some breakfast, Jake?"

Jake caught her hand and gave it a gentle squeeze.

"I'm fine. Really. Can we talk? I need to get back to the farm."

"Of course." She smiled, then caught the corner of her lip between her teeth. Reaching for the half-empty coffeepot, she refilled his cup. "Let's sit."

Tori pulled out a chair across from his, her expensive designer perfume wreathing him, jostling more imprisoned memories clamoring to be freed.

Feeling trapped, Jake had no choice but to oblige. The quicker they talked, the faster he could retreat to the farm.

Claudia sat between them, folded her arms on the table and looked at Jake. "I know why you're here."

"You do?"

"Yes, and it's not what you think." She covered his hand. "I'd never go back on my word, especially with your family."

"Then what's going on? When I stopped by the feed store, Gwen said your land had been sold."

"That woman needs to find better use of her time than spreading rumors and half-truths. After Dennis was diagnosed with cancer, we needed money for medical bills. Owning a business had its perks, but health insurance…well, that's a different kind of animal. I went behind my husband's back to see my brother, Frank. We haven't been close for many years, but I had no other choice—Dennis was my world. I sold the land and the house to Frank with the condition I'd have first option to buy it back should he choose to sell."

Jake clenched his teeth and forced himself to stay calm. "You should have come to us. We could've worked something out."

Claudia cupped his cheek and shook her head. "With

all you guys have been through with losing your mother, your dad's back surgery and rebuilding the farm after the tornado nearly destroyed everything? You had enough on your plate without my problems, especially after Tuck lost his wife... No, I couldn't burden you with this."

"But you're family, too."

"I just couldn't, okay? Besides, Frank came through for me. Dennis and I stayed on Holland Hill until he became too ill to keep up with the mowing and house maintenance. Moving into town allowed us to be closer to the hospital. In the year since he passed, I've been buried in grief and paperwork to get his life insurance checks. But before I could buy back the property, Frank passed away from a heart attack. Two months ago."

"I'm sorry." Jake glanced at Tori, who kept her gaze on her untouched coffee mug and traced the rim with her finger. "So that means..."

She looked at him, her eyes sad, yet almost...determined. "I own the property."

"You've got to be kidding."

"All of my father's assets have been divided between my sister and me. I'm now the owner of the house and property Aunt Claudia mentioned."

Jake jumped to his feet and paced. "Claudia..."

"When Dennis and I bought your grandparents' property after they passed away, we promised to give your family first dibs if we chose to sell it so it would never be sold outside the family. And it hasn't. So my promise is still intact."

Jake jerked a thumb toward Tori. "She's *your* family. Not mine."

Not anymore.

He ground his teeth together and forced breath into his lungs, then jerked his attention back to Tori. "I'd like to make an offer to buy that land."

She shook her head. "It's not for sale."

"What are you going to do with it?"

"I'm going to live there."

"You can't be serious."

"I am."

Claudia draped her arms around the two of them. "See? There's a silver lining in all of this. With the two of you being neighbors, I have the feeling you're going to hit it off right away. Oh, and not only that, but Tori can help you get your Fatigues to Farming project off the ground. She works in public relations."

Claudia couldn't be further from the truth. Jake needed that land to make good on a promise made years ago and to fix what he'd broken. He'd figure out another way because living down the road from Tori was something nightmares were made of.

And to work with her? Yeah, right. Forget that.

How was he supposed to survive being neighbors with the woman who didn't have the guts to face him when she ended their brief marriage six years ago?

Fresh starts came with a price. And Tori was about to pay hers.

If she'd taken two minutes to do some research before coming to Shelby Lake, she wouldn't have come face-to-face with the biggest regret of her life. How could she have forgotten where Jake was from?

The last six years had done little to detract from his good looks…or temper his anger.

Could she blame him, though?

What'd she expect? For him to take her in his arms and beg her not to leave again?

In her dreams, maybe.

Tori had no one to blame but herself. And she had to live with the consequences.

Now to convince Jake she wasn't a Disney villain and simply wanted a safe place to call home.

Where was that exactly?

Not in Pittsburgh anymore. If ever.

Even though she'd grown up with a roof over her head and food in her belly, she'd felt more like an uninvited guest than a wanted daughter. Her father may have met all of her material needs, but she would've taken his love over his money any day. She dreamed of having a family and a place where she belonged. Falling in love with Jake had given her security and the sense of belonging she craved, but that had been short-lived.

She pulled her Lexus into the dusty barnyard and idled while deciding where to look for him. A whitewashed cinder-block building with a metal roof and a large front window etched with Holland Family Farm sat in front of her. To her right, a newly built rustic barn with an evergreen-colored metal roof sat next to a silver silo and a white barn with metal siding. Hay fluttered down from the small second-story window of the rustic barn.

She'd start there.

Opening her door, she stepped out of her car. The humid air pasted her dress to her skin as the early afternoon sun beat down on her head. Wishing she'd thought to grab her sunglasses, Tori waved away the pesky black gnats swarming her face. She wrinkled her nose against the ripe smells of manure, freshly cut grass and warm milk, and sidestepped a suspicious-looking mud pile. Maybe she should've taken the time to change into something more appropriate before barreling after Jake.

Black-and-white cows in the shaded pasture across the road eyed her as they chewed their food and swatted at flies with their tails. A trail of chickens flapped and waddled along the white fencing separating the barnyard from a large two-story house shaded by a row of pines and a sturdy oak.

She stood in the expansive doorway, allowing her eyes a moment to adjust to the sudden decrease in lighting.

Country music blared from an old boom box resting on one of the rungs of a ladder that led to a loft. A heavy, thick rope, darkened with age, hung from one of the sturdy barn beams and swayed in the light breeze that blew through the building. The scent of new wood heated by the summer sun filled her nose.

"The barn's not much of a place for high heels and sundresses."

Tori swiveled to seek the source of Jake's voice. He appeared with a pitchfork in his hand. He'd stripped off his gray T-shirt and stood next to neatly stacked bales of hay in his faded jeans, grimy ball cap on backward, and worn leather gloves. His muscled chest was damp with sweat. He crossed to the old radio, flicked it off and leaned his pitchfork against the barn wall before retrieving his shirt hanging from a nail in the wall and pulling it over his head.

Was she relieved…or disappointed?

Forcing her eyes away, Tori glanced down at her sundress, toed off her heels and kicked them off to the side out of the way. "What are you doing?"

"Checking the roof and floor for any needed repairs, pitching old hay out the back window into the compost unit, and restacking some fresh stuff. You should've called." Jake reached for a bale and lifted it over his head to add to the growing stack.

"You're right. Sounds like you could use another hand."

"Sure, when there's one around." Jake jerked his hat off his head, pulled a navy bandanna from his back pocket and mopped his forehead. Pocketing the cloth, he righted his cap. "What are you doing here, Victoria?"

She hated the way he used her given name, laced with disdain and veiled anger…like her father used to.

"I wanted to apologize. I'm sorry my presence caught you off guard."

"Why today?" Jake yanked off his gloves and slapped them against his reddened palm. His eyes lifted and searched hers. "Why not yesterday? Or even to-morrow?"

The ragged edges of pain around the whisper in his voice sliced through her. "You remembered."

"Even though you filed for divorce less than three weeks after we were married, I will always remember our anniversary."

She dropped her gaze to the floor as her cheeks burned. With her big toe, she traced a circle in the dust. Tears pricked the backs of her eyes. "Jake…"

"Forget it, Tori. I'm not here to rehash the past. You've apologized. I accept. Now if you don't mind, I have work to do."

She ran a thumb and a forefinger under her eyes, probably smearing her eyeliner, and exhaled. "Aunt

Claudia told me about the tornado and how much you've lost. I'm so sorry."

"Thanks."

"She also mentioned your project. I can help."

"I don't need your help."

"You're a real one-man show, aren't you?"

"You know nothing about me anymore, so stop pretending you care."

"But I do care. I never stopped." Tori sat on a stray bale. The hay poked the backs of her legs. The pain was minor compared with the verbal barbs piercing her heart. "Tell me about your Fatigues to Farming project."

"The program will enable disabled vets to learn about farming so they can start their own small businesses."

"So how does my property tie in?"

He leaned the pitchfork against the ladder and reached for a water bottle on the floor. After taking a long drink, he wiped his mouth and looked at her. "Our property is necessary for growing crops and cow pastures. After Claudia and Dennis moved into town, we planned to buy back her property—it used to belong to my grandparents. We want to build accessible cabins for vets and their families to live in while they go through the program. Plus, there'd be space for a community garden."

"Would you consider a trade?"

His eyes narrowed. "What kind of trade?"

"My sister, Kendra, is deployed overseas, so I have temporary custody of her four-year-old daughter, Annabeth. We need a…safe place to live. Staying with Aunt Claudia isn't an option since her lease doesn't allow long-term guests. Help me get the house ready to move into, and you can use the rest of the acreage for your project."

"Sell it to me. Then you can have the money for something that won't need work."

"I don't want to sell."

"Why not?"

She raised her chin. "I have my reasons. That's my offer. How are you raising awareness for your program?"

"Haven't had time for that yet. Still working on grant paperwork. We need funds to get the program started."

"I've planned awareness campaigns for charities and different organizations. I could do a fund-raiser for you. And I'm good at what I do."

"At what cost?"

"No charge. A trade of services. It's a worthy cause, and I want to help."

Jake retrieved his gloves and slid them on. He reached for the pitchfork and headed to the back of the barn.

Tori tamped down the familiar feeling of rejection and walked over to where she'd kicked off her shoes. After sliding her feet back into them, she followed Jake. "You have twenty-four hours to think about it, then the offer's off the table."

He jammed the fork into a bale and glared at her. He threw his hands in the air as his voice rose. "Man, Tori. Give me a break, will you? I haven't heard from you in six years. You ignored my phone calls and letters when all I wanted was the answer to one simple question—why? Instead of hearing from you, I get divorce papers handed to me through my commanding officer with orders not to contact you or else face charges. So excuse me for being a little gun-shy."

"I'm sorry. That's not how I wanted things to happen."

"You didn't stop it."

Tori crossed to the open window that overlooked the barnyard. Tears blurred her vision as her voice dropped to a whisper. "I couldn't."

Unwelcome memories swirled in her head, tangling with her thoughts and roping her emotions. She didn't want to remember the pain ripping through her body or hear the whine of the ambulance as it rushed her to the hospital. Or relive the sympathetic tone of the doctor as he broke the news. Or the convincing tone in her father's voice as he tried to suggest he had only her best interests at heart.

Tell him.

Not here. Not now.

"Couldn't? Or wouldn't?" Jake stood behind her.

She whirled around, fisted her hands on her hips, then poked a finger into his chest. "These last six years haven't been a picnic for me either. There's so much you don't know. If I could change the past, I would. Since I can't, all I can do is make a fresh start. A safe place to care for my niece while her mother finishes her deployment, and maybe, if it's not asking too much, a chance to make amends. I'm sorry I hurt you, Jake. It was wrong, and I regret it more than anything. But I've lost a lot, too." She brushed past him and caught her foot, turning her ankle. Pain lanced her leg. She reached down and rubbed her throbbing joint. "You were right about one thing, the barn is no place for a sundress and high heels. Twenty-four hours. You know where to find me."

"Wait."

She stopped, keeping her back to him. The fatigue in his voice nearly unraveled her. More than anything, she wanted to wrap her arms around him, but that was impossible. He didn't want her around, let alone to be touched by her. She clenched her jaw, mentally preparing for another round.

"Be here at nine thirty tomorrow morning. And wear something more appropriate for getting dirty."

Tori nodded, headed out the door and stomped back to her car.

Like it or not, Jacob Holland, she was sticking around.

Even though she knew it couldn't be, her heart longed for that second chance.

To fix what she'd broken. But that wasn't possible.

Because once he learned the truth—what they'd truly lost—he'd want nothing to do with her again. But, for now, she wasn't ready to risk being out of his life forever. So she'd stay and prove she was good at keeping her word this time—with the wild hope it didn't destroy them both. Again.

Chapter Two

Jake needed to have his head examined. Why did he tell Tori to be here this morning? Hadn't he been tortured enough with seeing her yesterday?

But this wasn't about him.

He'd suck it up, even if that meant spending time with the one woman he longed to forget.

Like that was even possible.

Jake finished hosing down the floor inside the milk house, directing the water toward the drain under the milk tank. Wiping his hands on the legs of his jeans, he grabbed his empty travel mug, headed outside and breathed in a lungful of cool morning air—a welcoming contrast to the warm, steamy milk house—and allowed the breeze to whisk over his sweaty face.

A line of chickens clucked as they hurried to the coop next to the milk barn. Cows lumbered for the shade trees in the pasture across the road. Soon, his niece and nephew would be awake, and then there wouldn't be any quiet until bedtime. Not that Jake cared. He loved hanging out with Olivia and Landon.

Cuddles, a butterscotch-colored barn cat his niece

had named, curled around his ankles. Jake scooped her up. Purring, she nuzzled his neck. "Good morning, Mama. Where are your kittens?"

He glanced at the open barn door and found the three kittens batting at each other. Jake put her down and cut across the backyard to the farmhouse. He needed breakfast and coffee before facing Tori.

Lots of coffee.

He took the back deck steps two at a time and paused outside the back door to remove his barn boots.

Even though Mom had been gone for five years, her rules remained. And that meant no barn boots in the house.

Scents of fresh-brewed coffee mingling with fried bacon greeted him as he stepped into the kitchen.

Still dressed in his blue paramedic's uniform, Tucker, his younger brother by a year, stood at the stove, turning home fries in a cast-iron skillet. "Hey, man. Grab a plate. Your food's ready."

Jake did as directed, handed the plate to his brother and then reached for the coffeepot to refill his travel mug. "Thanks, brother."

"Anytime."

Taking the food and the coffee to the large oak table, Jake sat and bowed his head, uttering a quick, silent prayer. Another one of Mom's rules—always be thankful for what you're given.

His eyes skimmed across the hand-painted sign hanging above the farmhouse sink. *In every thing give thanks.*

Would Mom still feel that way if she knew what the future held for the Holland family?

After losing so much, Jake struggled with thankfulness. He went through the motions of praying and attending church, but he doubted his prayers reached past the ceiling. Didn't matter that he could recite verses from memory, list the books of the Bible and answer trivia questions with the best of them. He and God... well, they were more like strangers these days.

How could he have a meaningful relationship with Someone who took the people he loved most?

His eyes strayed to Dad's open Bible on the table in his usual spot. More often than not, he'd walk into the farmhouse after milking and see Dad with his reading glasses on, Bible open and a cup of coffee in his hand.

How did Dad and Tuck maintain their faith without feeling resentful? How could it be God's will to destroy a family?

Questions without answers. And Jake struggled to wrap his head around it.

He dropped his gaze to the pile of steaming eggs and shoved a forkful in his mouth. He ate half a slice of rye toast in two bites and washed it down with a mouthful of coffee.

Tucker snapped his fingers in front of Jake's face. "Hey, man. Wake up. Claudia's here."

Terrific.

Jake stifled a sigh, looked longingly at the rest of his breakfast and palmed his travel mug as he pushed away from the table. "Hold onto my plate, will you? I'll finish it later."

"Where are you going?"

"To the barn. I'm giving Claudia's niece a tour of the farm."

"Enjoy."

Not likely.

Jake scooted out the back door, shoved his feet into his boots and headed for the barnyard.

Perhaps the polite thing would've been to greet Claudia and Tori at the front door and show Tori where to go, but he was sure Dad would take care of that.

It gave him a couple of extra minutes to psych himself into seeing Tori again.

He headed into the barn, gathered the saddles and pads, and carried them out to the yard, hanging them on the fence. Returning to the barn, he grabbed the bridles and fetched Westley and Buttercup, two buckskin quarter horses, and led them out of the barn as Tori crossed the yard to meet him. She carried a small brown bag in one hand while her niece, wearing denim shorts and a pink T-shirt, clutched her other hand.

Tori wore a light blue fitted T-shirt with a yellow cup and Luke's printed on it. Jeans hugged her legs, and she wore a pair of gray outdoor hiking sandals. She'd pulled her hair back into a ponytail that flopped as she walked.

They reached the fence where the lawn hemmed the barnyard. The little girl looked at Jake with clover-green eyes like Tori's and the same crease in her cheeks when she smiled.

Jake's heart ratcheted against his ribs.

That child could pass for Tori's daughter.

What would it have been like to have a child with Tori? A little girl with those same eyes and dimples? A boy with his dark hair and love of animals?

Jake chased away that thought. Dangerous territory.

Tori lifted the little girl in her arms. "Annabeth wanted to see the animals, so your dad and Claudia are going to show her the pigs and chickens while I tour your farm with you."

He stuck out his hand. "Hey, Annabeth. It's nice to see you again. My name's Jake."

She buried her face in Tori's shoulder, then turned to give him a shy smile.

Tori kissed her on the cheek, then set her down. "Why don't you run back to the house and see if Auntie C is ready to see the piggies."

Annabeth ran across the yard, then turned back and gave them a little wave.

"She's cute."

"Yes, she is." She handed him a brown lunch bag.

He took it, eying the grease stain on the bag. "What's this?"

"Peace offering."

He opened the bag to find two golden-topped biscuits. He reached for one, surprised to find it still warm, and took a bite. Butter rolled across his tongue. He swallowed a groan and took another bite.

Hands clasped in front of her, Tori bit the corner of her lip as she watched him.

Jake finished off the biscuit, licked the melted butter off his fingers and reached for his travel mug sitting on a fence post. "Thank you. That was…good."

"Really?" Tori smiled. "I'm glad you liked it."

"I haven't had biscuits like that since Mom…well, in a long time."

Tori wrapped her arms around her waist. "Actually, I made them using your mom's recipe that Aunt Claudia had."

"You made these?" Jake held up the bag. "But…" Jake's voice trailed off. No sense in bringing up the past.

"I know. I used to burn toast. But I'm not that same

girl anymore, Jake." She searched his face, almost as if she was begging him to believe her.

Jake stared at her, feeling himself being pulled in by those eyes. He drank in her smooth skin, the faint sprinkle of freckles she always tried to cover with makeup and her parted bare lips.

The wind toyed with the stray hairs, brushing them across her cheek.

He fisted his hand to keep from touching her.

Westley nickered and pawed the dirt, jerking Jake's attention away from Tori.

He scrubbed a hand over his face and reached for the saddle pad he'd laid over the fence. He carried it over to Buttercup and smoothed it over her back. He ran a hand over her neck, and then he looked at Tori. "Mind checking out the farm on horseback?"

"Kind of late to be asking that, aren't you?" She tossed him a grin and reached for the saddle. She carried it over to Buttercup, rested it on the horse's back, then made quick work of cinching the girth straps. She dusted off her knees and petted the horse. "Thanks to the summer camps my father sent me to, I can hold my own."

Jake checked the tightness.

Tori rested a hand on his forearm. "Jake, I've been riding since I was a kid. I know what I'm doing."

Reaching for the pommel, Tori put her foot in the stirrup and pulled herself into the saddle. The leather creaked as she seated herself. Buttercup back-stepped and nickered against the weight, tossing her mane. Tori leaned forward, whispered something in the horse's ear and patted the side of her neck.

Jake saddled Westley and mounted the horse. "Westley and Buttercup were my parents' horses. Dad can't ride anymore and with Mom gone, they don't get exercised as much as they should."

One more thing to add to his growing to-do list.

"*Princess Bride* fans, huh?"

"Mom's favorite movie." Leading them out of the barnyard, Jake guided them to the side of the road. Traffic wouldn't be a problem. Another reason he loved Holland Hill.

As they passed a worn, weathered red barn that sat between the farm and Tori's property, she slowed Buttercup.

"Problem?"

She shook her head and pointed at the barn. "What's that used for?"

"Nothing anymore. Well, not livestock. It's the first barn my grandfather built and the only one to weather the tornado. Now it's used mainly for storage."

"Can I see it?"

Jake shrugged. "Sure."

They dismounted, then he opened the fence to the pasture behind the barn for the horses to graze while he and Tori walked up the barn bridge and stood in the expansive doorway. Wings flapped from the rafters. Streams of sunshine beamed through the open windows to shine spotlights on the old wooden floor.

Tori stood under the loft and checked out the rafters. She turned to him with a grin. "What would you say to an old-fashioned barn dance?"

"Barn dance? For what?"

"A fund-raiser for your program. The best place to host an awareness campaign for your program would be on the property where it's going to take place. Let's bring people to Holland Hill. I'm picturing a small petting zoo for the kids, hayrides, a barbecue, perhaps an auction of items donated by local businesses, and end the evening with a barn dance right here. And if you were feeling adventurous, we could look into fireworks."

"No fireworks, especially with veterans who can still hear the artillery fire in their heads when the rest of the world is quiet."

"Sorry. I didn't think of that."

"And people would be willing to pay to attend?" Jake shot her his best "you can't be serious" look, but she merely grinned.

"Of course, especially once they hear about the program. We'll presell tickets so we have a general idea of how many people to expect. We'll get vendors to give us discounts or even free products in exchange for advertising." As she talked, Tori continued to examine the barn. "If your family wanted to branch out, this barn would be perfect for rustic weddings and receptions. Brides are into that kind of thing these days."

Jake gave her a look like he had no clue what she was talking about.

"Just think about using the barn. Aunt Claudia mentioned how much you valued your privacy, but I believe hosting the fund-raiser here will give people an authentic view of your vision. People will invest in programs they can get behind."

"After the tornado, we had all kinds of news crews up and down the hill. So, yeah, we do like our privacy, but I do hear what you're saying. I'll have to talk to Dad and Tuck."

They headed to the pasture. Jake opened the fence

and whistled. Westley and Buttercup trotted over to him, and he grabbed their reins.

"Let me know what you decide. In the meantime, I can put together some notes for you to share with them." Tori mounted Buttercup and nodded down the road. "My house is right there. Want to stop by and see what needs to be done?"

The way Tori sat in the saddle released a memory of when they rode together on the beach during their weekend honeymoon. Did she remember? He wasn't about to ask and head down that path. He glanced at his watch and shook his head. "Sorry. Can't. I need to get some stuff done in the barn before heading to the fields. Another time?"

"Sure. No problem."

Despite her smile, Tori's voice sounded like she didn't believe him, but she could think what she wanted. He had chores to do, but he could've pushed them back another hour. Truth was, he needed a break. Even though they managed to spend time together without bickering, he realized how easy it would be to get caught up in her charms. He couldn't risk that again. Not when there was much more at stake this time. He needed to keep his focus on the program.

Tori was in over her head.

What made her think she could give up the city life and live in the country?

Sure, she could handle the ten-minute drive into Shelby Lake for a good cup of coffee. And she certainly didn't mind the lack of traffic. Or even the smells that drifted downwind from the Holland Farm.

But, seriously, could she spend a lifetime living down

the road from a man who wanted nothing to do with her? Again, she had no one to blame but herself. And it didn't help that she'd sat up half the night making notes about Jake's program. Maybe once he saw what she was capable of doing, he'd see the value in having her around.

But she needed to stop dwelling on Jake and make good use of the two kid-free hours she had to work on the house.

When Aunt Claudia offered to take Annabeth to the park with her grandchildren, Tori wasted no time in making a list. She always worked better with a plan.

Grabbing her phone and water bottle, she headed for the staircase to check out the second-floor bedrooms. If she could get those, the bathroom and the kitchen in working order, then she and Annabeth could move in sooner, then work on the other rooms as time and money allowed.

Aunt Claudia confessed to lacking the motivation to keep up the house once her husband had gotten sick and they moved into town. Hopefully, any work needing to be done was cosmetic and wouldn't eat up her entire savings.

As she climbed the steps, Tori sucked in a breath as her thigh muscles quivered and protested each movement.

Did Jake suggest a horseback farm tour to see if she could handle it?

She'd ridden horses before. Lots of times. But she hadn't been on one since…well, their honeymoon and the ride they'd taken on the beach.

Had he remembered? If so, he'd given no inclination. Not that she expected him to.

At the top of the stairs, Tori scanned the small sitting area with a window that overlooked the backyard. She pictured a couple of cushy chairs with knitted afghans, a filled bookcase, a reading lamp and a patterned throw rug to soften the original hardwood floor. The faded yellow walls needed to be repainted. After dictating a few notes into her phone, she checked out each of the three bedrooms with identical hardwood floors. Thankfully, they needed nothing more than to be cleaned and repainted.

The bathroom was another matter. Sure, she could live with the aqua-colored tub and matching toilet and black linoleum and call it retro, but did she want to? Replacing them would put quite a dent in her savings.

What had Aunt Claudia been thinking by keeping the decades-old fixtures?

After snapping a few photos and taking more notes, Tori headed out of the room and noticed a door outside the bathroom at the top of the stairs. How had she missed that coming up? Probably because she'd been too busy whining to herself about climbing the Mount Everest steps.

Must be a linen closet.

She tried to turn the old-fashioned black knob, but it was tight. She turned harder, and the door popped open. She made a quick note to replace the knob and tucked the phone in the back pocket of her jeans.

Definitely not a closet. It had to be the entrance to the attic Aunt Claudia had mentioned. Tori had expected a pull-down set of rickety steps.

She peered up the steps, seeing nothing but shadows. Was she brave enough to venture into the unknown? And climb more stairs?

She felt the wall for a light switch and flicked it on before remembering the utilities hadn't been turned on yet. Another thing to add to her to-do list.

A heavy musty odor hung over the darkness like an invisible curtain. Light filtered through a dirty rectangular window at the top of the stairs, casting shadows across dusty rafters and various-sized boxes.

Maybe she could open the window to air out the space.

Tori pulled her phone out and flicked on the flashlight, pointing it ahead of her. Dust motes danced in the narrow beam. The low-battery warning chimed. She'd have to hurry.

Cobwebs, burdened with dust, stretched between sturdy beams. The wooden floor creaked beneath her feet as she made her way to the window. She felt like she'd stepped inside a Nancy Drew novel, exploring with Nancy, George and Bess.

Something rustled to her right.

Tori froze, her heart hammering against her rib cage.

Maybe she didn't need to open the window after all.

Pointing her phone in the direction of the noise, she flashed the light across a rusted metal tool chest, half a dozen boxes, stray limbs from an artificial Christmas tree and a plastic play kitchen missing a faucet.

She exhaled and shook her head.

Nothing to be afraid of.

Something soft and furry brushed against her ankle, and Tori yelped, jumping back. She shined the light to the floor as a tiny gray puff with a long tail scampered across her foot and disappeared into the darkness.

She screamed, dropped her phone and turned, slamming her toe against the metal toolbox. Pain shot across her foot.

Clenching her jaw to hold back another scream, Tori snatched her phone off the floor and half ran, half limped to the doorway.

She hurried down the stairs to find the door had closed behind her. She hadn't even heard it. She twisted the tight knob, but it wouldn't budge.

Oh. Come. On.

She rammed her shoulder against the door. She tried the knob one more time, turning with all the strength she could manage. She felt a pop, but instead of the door opening, the stupid knob broke off in her hand.

Terrific.

What was she going to do now?

Tori plopped down on the step and tossed the knob next to her. It clattered down the two stairs and rolled against the stuck door.

She sucked in a deep breath. Sweat beaded across her forehead as a chill stroked her arms. She gathered her knees to her chest and closed her eyes, focusing on slow, even breaths.

Think, Victoria.

There had to be some way of getting the door open.

Tiny feet scurried across the floor above her.

And soon.

Maybe the wretched toolbox she stubbed her toe against had a screwdriver or something in it.

She reached for her phone, turned on her music and blasted the volume as she limped back up the steps and flashed the light to guide her. She found the toolbox, reached for the latch and felt a small padlock.

Of course.

Her phone beeped, then dimmed in her hand.

She headed for the stairs while she had enough light to guide her path. She took another step, and the floor gave slightly, feeling a bit spongy. As she took one more step, her foot slid on a slick spot. She reached out to catch herself and dropped the phone, plunging her into darkness except for the light coming from the grimy window.

Her weight landed on her right side, forcing her foot through the damaged floorboard. She tried to pull her foot free, but pain knifed her ankle.

Tori's chest shuddered as her breathing quickened and her pulse raced.

She was trapped with no way of calling for help. Darkness hooded her as the noises amplified.

Was that a squeak?

Something brushed against her arm. She batted at it.

She was back in the closet again. In her father's house. But this time she wasn't cradling a terrified Annabeth against her chest, trying to silence the little girl's sobs so they wouldn't be found by intruders plowing through the downstairs.

No.

She was safe.

In her own house.

But trapped.

Branches scratched against the windowpane, throwing long-fingered shadows across the room…reaching out for her. With no phone, how was she going to be able to call Aunt Claudia for help?

Help me, God.

Seconds became minutes.

Tires crunched in the driveway. A moment later, the

doorbell rang. Then someone pounded on the door, calling her name.

Why had she locked the door?

Because she was a scaredy-cat.

A grown woman afraid to be in the house by herself. And of the dark.

A moment later, an engine started.

"No! Don't leave! Help me!" Tori's cries, punctuated by sobs, bounced off the beams.

She tried to pull her foot free again and sucked in a sharp breath as the splintered wood razored her leg. She dropped to the floor and tried to pry the damaged wood away, but it broke off in pieces. A splinter speared her finger.

Heavy footsteps thundered up the staircase to the second floor.

Someone *was* in her house.

Tori brushed a hand over her face. "Help!"

Wood splintered with a loud crack, then swung free, throwing welcoming light up the darkened steps.

"Tori?" Jake's voice caused fresh tears to fill Tori's eyes.

She blinked them back. "I'm up here. My foot is stuck."

He raced up the steps and swung a flashlight in her direction.

She threw up a hand to shield against the brightness. Jake hurried over to her. Handing her the flashlight, he knelt beside her. "Hold this."

His gentle touch pressed against her bruised flesh as he worked a large enough area to pull her foot free from the rotted board. "There you go. You're free."

Jake cupped her elbow and helped her to stand.

Tori launched herself into his arms, nearly knocking him off balance. "Get me out of here."

Jake scooped her into his arms and carried her down the steps, through the house and out the front door, where he deposited her gently on the top step of the front porch.

Tori gulped in a lungful of fresh air, wiped the backs of her hands across the dried trail of tears down her cheeks and forced a smile. "I'm not a damsel in distress, you know. I *can* take care of myself."

"Everyone needs to be rescued at one point or another, and there's no shame in that." Jake looked at her a moment, then jerked a thumb over his shoulder toward his truck. "I have a first aid kit in the glove box. Let me grab it and clean up your leg a little."

He returned a moment later and tore open an antiseptic wipe as she pulled up the leg of her jeans. Gritting her teeth, she tensed as the antiseptic wipe stung the cut above her ankle.

"Sorry." He shot her a quick look. "What happened?"

Tori gave him a replay and tried not to wince as his fingers brushed across the torn skin. After cleaning the area, he ripped open three bandages and plastered them over the cut. "I don't think it's deep enough for stitches, but you can get it checked out if you want. Or I can have Tuck look it over once he wakes up—he works midnights."

"I trust you. It's just a cut. Nothing serious." Tori reached for her phone but found her back pocket to be empty. Oh, that's right—it had flown out of her hand. She heaved a sigh, causing Jake's eyes to jerk to her face.

"You okay?"

She dragged a hand over her face and pressed it to her throbbing forehead. "My phone. It's lost in the attic somewhere. Aunt C's going to wonder where I am. How did you know I was here anyway?"

"I drove by, saw your car and decided to stop for a quick tour of the house to see what needs to be done. Looks like we'll have to start by patching that hole." Jake shot her a half smile that sent her heart skittering across her ribs. He gathered the trash, stuffed it into his front pocket and closed the first aid kit. "Are you okay to drive?"

"Of course. It's nothing more than a bruise and a cut."

He held out his hand to her. "Lean on me. I'll get you to your car so you can rest for a moment, then I'll go back to the attic to find your phone."

Lean on me.

She'd love nothing more.

Jake wrapped an arm around her waist and guided her down the steps. She pressed her cheek into the softness of his T-shirt and inhaled the scent of hay mixed with sunshine. For the first time in a very long time, she felt safe. But knowing it was a momentary kindness—of Jake being Jake and helping out someone in need—filled her heart with sadness that threatened to buckle her knees.

She wanted his forgiveness. A fresh start. But that wasn't possible. He'd made that clear already. And somehow she had to figure out how to live with that.

Chapter Three

Finding Tori trapped and terrified in her attic knifed Jake in the gut.

Not to mention the way she'd clung to him after he'd freed her foot. Hearing her cries and feeling her trembling shook him more than he cared to admit.

Not wanting her to go through that again, he'd insisted she get the utilities transferred into her name and turned on. If he was going to work on her house, he needed power for his tools anyway.

And with rain soaking the fields, today seemed like the perfect time to get started. The sooner, the better, especially with rotted floorboards in the attic.

Jake shined his flashlight across the damaged floor. White fungus stained the dark wood. He pulled at one of the ragged edges and it flaked off in his hand.

Definitely dry rot.

The attic floorboards would need to be replaced, which meant a trip to the home improvement store.

He straightened, pulled off his leather gloves and brushed dirt off his knees. A drop of water splatted his forehead and slid between his eyes. He shined his light across the ceiling and found a bubble of water between two wet rafters.

He was afraid of that. A leaking roof wasn't something to ignore.

Did Tori's budget include roof replacement?

Probably not, but they'd have to make it happen if she wanted to live here.

But repairing the roof would have to wait until the rain stopped. He needed to find a sheet of plywood to cover the hole in the floor for now and grab a bucket or something to catch the water.

He headed for the staircase to find Tori standing in the doorway to the attic with her hands pressed against the walls and one foot on the first step. "Hey, I was coming to find you."

"What's up?"

"I said your family could use my property, but I didn't expect to find cows in my backyard."

"What are you talking about?"

"I was washing walls in the back bedroom when I heard mooing. I looked out and found them in the backyard."

Jake hurried down the steps, brushed past her and rushed into the bedroom that smelled like lemon cleaner. A glance out the sparkling window showed half a dozen heifers grazing in her grass.

Why weren't they bedded down in the barn?

He pulled out his phone and tapped on Tucker's name. When the call went to his brother's voice mail, Jake called the farmhouse. "Hey, Dad, is Tuck around?"

"No, he took the twins to the dentist. Need something?"

"Cows are out. I was going to have him give me a hand to round them up."

"I'll help. Where are you?"

"I'm at Tori's, but you stay put. No sense in both of us getting wet. I'll take care of it." Jake ended the call, stowed his phone and looked at Tori. "Sorry, but I gotta go."

"I can help you."

Jake eyed her thin yellow T-shirt layered over a tank top or something, cutoff shorts fraying around the edges and flowered flip-flops. "I'll handle it."

"Hypocrite."

"What'd you call me?"

"You heard me. You're so afraid of letting people help that you shoulder all the burdens by yourself."

Jake tossed his hands in the air. "Fear has nothing to do with it. Dad's recovering from back surgery. Tuck's at the dentist with his kids. Evan and Micah are doing their own thing. Looks like I'm the only guy to do the work."

"*I* just offered."

"What do you know about herding cows?" Jake headed for the stairs.

She followed behind him. "Not a thing, but I can follow directions well. And, right now, it seems like you could use an extra set of hands."

He'd done things on his own for so long that he didn't know how to ask for…or accept help. Not only that, but he couldn't risk something happening to someone else he cared about.

Whoa.

The traitorous thought slammed into his chest like one of his 1,500-pound heifers.

He cared about Tori? After what she'd done?

Not by choice.

He preferred to feel indifferent. That way, every word, every moment, every glimpse of her didn't set his heart on fire.

Truth was, she'd been here only a handful of days and she was getting under his skin. Again.

Jake strode through the kitchen for the back door, trying to ignore the person close enough to be his shadow.

The rain slowed to a mist, creating steamy, humid air that stirred up scents of plowed earth, freshly cut grass and wet animals.

One of the cows eyed him from under the apple tree and bawled.

Jake reached in his pocket, pulled out the farm truck keys and handed them to Tori. "If you want to help, drive the truck to the barn. I need to load fencing supplies."

She took the keys without a word and rounded the side of the house to the driveway.

He strode across the wet grass to one of the heifers and ran a hand over her damp hide. "Hey, don't cry to me. You're the ones who left the barn to stand in the rain. Time to head back inside."

He jogged across the yard to get in front of the wayward herd and turned to face them. Cupping his hands around his mouth, he called, "Come on, cows. Come on."

They responded to his voice with mooing, but they ambled toward him with the speed of Sunday afternoon drivers. As they passed the fence, Jake noticed a heavy limb on the ground between two posts. Mystery solved as to how they got out. Within minutes, Jake led them back into the barn and secured the gate across the doorway, which allowed for fresh air but prevented another escape.

Tori had parked in the barnyard and left the truck idling. He motioned for her to drive to the white utility barn, where he loaded a chain saw, roll of barbed wire, fence stretcher and barbed wire pliers. He opened the passenger door and hopped inside.

"Where to now?"

"Back to your place. I'll drop you off, then I'll drive into the pasture to fix the fence."

"Tell me where to go. I can help."

He laughed. "Fixed a lot of fences, have you, city girl?"

She shot him a glare. "Not a single one, but like I said earlier, I follow directions well and you could use another set of hands, country boy."

He swallowed a reply and turned up the radio, then regretted it. A current hit about love that was meant to be filled the cab.

Not for him. Not again.

Jake lowered the window, rested an elbow on the door frame, and rubbed his tired eyes with his thumb and index finger.

It wasn't that he didn't appreciate Tori's help. Anyone else, and he'd jump at the chance for extra hands.

But, Tori…man, being around her so much was killing him. Every time she moved, he breathed in her expensive perfume that rattled memories that needed to stay locked up. At one time, he would've given almost anything to hear her voice once again, the softness of her lips against his, her silky hair through his fingers…

But, no. They were *not* meant to be.

The broken fence came into view. "Pull up to the fence where that heavy limb is lying. The lightning must have hit the tree, and the noise spooked the cows, which caused them to bolt."

She did as instructed and shut off the engine. "Does that happen a lot?"

"Cows getting out? More than any farmer would like. Fences require consistent checking and maintenance, and we're in the process of replacing all the fencing. I do what I can but..." His growing to-do list weighed on his shoulders. Jake shook it off, hopped out of the truck and opened the back door to the extended cab. He searched for some gloves. He found one pair wedged between the seats, but where were the leather ones he'd used earlier?

Still in Tori's attic.

He'd removed them while inspecting the floorboards and hadn't picked them up before heading downstairs.

Perfect.

Well, he'd handled fencing all his life, so he'd simply be careful.

"Put these on to protect your hands." He tossed her the gloves, then closed the doors. He reached over the tailgate for the chain saw. A few minutes later, the downed limb lay in chunks on the ground. Perfect size for firewood.

He returned to the truck, stowed the chain saw, shoved the fencing pliers in his back pocket, handed the rusty yellow fence stretcher that had been his grandfather's to Tori and reached for the roll of wire, careful not to snag it on his skin. He jerked his head toward the fence. "Follow me."

Jake set the roll on the ground where lines of loose wire sagged between two posts. He knelt between them, soaking the knees of his jeans, and picked up one end of the broken wire, twisting it into a loop. Reaching for the roll of wire, he ran the free end in through the loop and wrapped it a few times to secure it. Jake picked up the other end of the broken wire, bent it around the head of the fencing pliers and twisted it into a loop. He scanned the ground for the fence stretcher and realized Tori still held it.

She'd been so quiet. For a moment, he'd forgotten she was there. But now knowing she watched his movements sent the hairs on the back of his neck standing at attention. He held out a hand. "May I have that, please?"

She handed it to him and knelt beside him.

"Careful. There are prickers in the grass." Jake seated the wires in the grooves and clamped them. "Remember the old ratchet car jacks?"

She stared at him with a blank look, then shrugged as pink brightened her cheeks. "No, not really."

He smiled. "No big deal. Well, the fence stretcher uses that same ratchet motion to tighten the wires. Want to try it out?"

"What do I do?" She reached for it, her hand brushing against his.

"Just grab this handle and move it back and forth. It travels along this grooved edge and pulls the two sections of wire together." Jake moved behind her, covered her hands and demonstrated the pumping action required to move the tool.

She did as instructed as Jake stepped back.

The sound of metal snapping jerked Jake's attention away from Tori's gloved hands to the wire jumping free of the stretcher. He grabbed onto it, preventing it from slicing her face.

Pain flared through his hand as the barb flayed his palm. Crimson stained his skin and raced between his fingers.

"Jake!" Tori dropped the fence stretcher, tore off her gloves and pulled off her T-shirt, revealing a cream-colored, lace-edged camisole. She wrapped the shirt around his hand, causing him to cry out. "Sorrysorry-sorry! We need to get you to the ER."

Jake wanted to argue, but the searing pain scrambled his brains.

Tori guided him to the truck, then slid in behind the wheel. Her fingers shook as she tried to start the engine.

Jake pressed his head against the seat rest, closed his eyes, and forced air in and out of his lungs.

He deserved a swift kick. Why didn't he make sure the wire had been seated correctly before clamping it down? What was he thinking?

Problem was, when Tori was around, thinking went out the window.

He knew better than to grab the wire without gloves, but seeing it springing toward Tori's face...

And now he won a trip to the ER for his lack of focus. *Way to go, hotshot.*

If Tori hadn't insisted on helping Jake, then he wouldn't be on the couch snoring softly under the influence of pain meds prescribed after his unexpected surgery to repair the flexor tendon in his right hand.

One more thing for him to hold against her.

She hated his carrying everyone's burdens, and with

all the help he'd given her, if she could give back even a little, then maybe she could redeem herself.

Tori picked up her iPad and tried to focus on the fund-raising notes she'd been making about Jake's project. She'd gotten a list of local businesses and started a letter requesting sponsorship, but she couldn't give it the proper attention.

Instead, her eyes roamed across the room, over the framed family photos hanging on barn board walls—the boys' graduation, Jake's and Micah's boot camp photos, Tucker with his twins as infants, Evan holding a kayak paddle in one hand and a trophy in the other. The flat-screen TV hung above the brick fireplace that begged to be lit. Piles of farming magazines lay scattered on the square wooden coffee table nicked with scars and white water rings. Brownish leaves on the tall plant in the corner showed it thirsted for light and water. Tan tabbed curtains had been drawn to keep out the sunshine heating the bay window.

Her gaze settled on Jake. Sprawled on the dark brown leather couch, he slept on his back with his left arm over his head and his splinted, bandaged right hand resting on his chest. The cream-colored chunky knitted afghan had fallen to the floor, leaving Jake exposed in a navy blue T-shirt and khaki cargo shorts with a torn pocket.

His face softened under the necessity of rest. The furrowed brows relaxed. The lines around his mouth disappeared in the shadow of his scuff. She longed to run her fingers through his hair, brush the stray strands off his tanned forehead. But it wasn't her place.

She set her tablet on the arm of the matching over-stuffed chair where she'd been sitting and stood. Clasping her hands together and lifting her arms above her head, she stretched and rolled the kinks from her neck.

Jake groaned and mumbled something, but Tori couldn't make out his words. Scowling, he shook his head. Beneath his eyelids, his eyes darted back and forth. He circled his arms in front of him, almost as if trying to grab onto something. "Tori! No!"

He jerked awake, his chest heaving and breathing ragged. His eyes found hers, and she took a step toward him, then stopped. "What are you doing here?"

"Keeping an eye on you." He was dreaming about her? Sounded more like a nightmare.

"I don't need a babysitter." Jake sat up and moved to the edge of the couch. He rested both elbows on his knees, cradled his injured hand against his chest and dragged his other hand across his face, then through his hair. "Feel free to leave. I'm fine."

"You had surgery yesterday."

"You're not my wife anymore, Tori. You don't belong here." He stood and left the room.

His sharp words lashed at her heart with the chill of a frosty winter morning, turning her skin cold. He voiced the things she'd been turning over in her head. But she promised Jake's father, Chuck, she'd hang around, and that's what she was going to do whether Jake liked it or not.

He returned a moment later with a full glass of water and stopped short as if surprised to see her. He set the glass on the table, sloshing water onto one of the magazines. She reached for a tissue from the box on the table next to the chair and mopped up the water.

Jake reached for her hand. "Stop. You don't need to clean up my messes. I'm serious."

Tori balled the soggy tissue in her hand and resisted the urge to throw it at him. "Listen, Jake—"

"No, *you* listen. This is my house. The one place where I can go for a little peace and quiet. Just…leave."

"No. Your dad asked me to stay until he got back, and that's what I'm going to do. I'm sure the pain in your hand is causing you to act like a jerk, so I'll try not to get all sensitive female on you and crumble into a weeping ball because you hurt my feelings."

"Fine. Whatever. Do what you want. You're good at that." He reached for the remote and flicked through soap operas, daytime talk shows and home shopping, finally settling on a black-and-white Western. Two minutes into the program, he flicked it off and tossed the remote onto the cushion beside him. "Where's Dad anyway?"

"Claudia drove him to an appointment."

"I thought Tucker was doing that."

"Tucker and the twins are at the barn. A milk inspector or someone like that showed up a little bit ago."

Jake's eyes widened. "Are you serious?" Then he buried his face in his good hand. "Oh, man. I left a mess in the milk house I'd planned to take care of yesterday."

"It's been taken care of."

"What are you talking about?"

"One of the neighboring farmers called your dad yesterday and mentioned a rumor of the milk inspector in the area. Claudia and I watched the twins while he and Tuck hung out at the hospital during your surgery, but then Tuck asked if we could watch them a little longer so he could make sure the milk house was ready to go."

"I should've been there. It was my mess, my responsibility to clean it up."

"You need to chill out. Everything's under control."

"No, it's not, Victoria. Everything's falling apart." He waved his bandaged hand, then winced. "This... this is ridiculous. How can I do my job with a hand I can't use for...what? Like six weeks or something crazy like that?"

She picked at the piece of skin on the side of her thumb, hating the way he emphasized her given name. Stripped it down until it left her feeling raw and wounded like her hangnail. She leveled him with a direct look. "Your hand will heal, Jake. In the meantime, it's okay to ask for help."

He paced in front of the fireplace. "There is no one else."

"I can help." She moved to the window and pulled back the curtains, flooding the room with the light it craved.

"Like you helped with fixing the fence?"

"Feel free to blame me. I'm a big girl. I can take it, but remember—all I did was follow *your* directions."

"You're a distraction, Tori." His shoulders sagged as he sat on the edge of the couch, his voice dropping to a whisper. "A distraction that costs too much."

For once in her life, she wanted to be worth that cost to someone who valued her enough to want to keep her around, to want to be distracted by her presence.

Jake reached for his glass and nearly dropped it. "This is really inconvenient."

"Imagine how those veterans you want to help feel." Tori picked up her iPad and sat next to him. "You're inconvenienced for a few weeks, but their abilities have been compromised for the rest of their lives. Some of them are learning to use artificial limbs. Maybe it's time to stop your pity party and gain some perspective."

He blew out a breath and reached for his glass, steadier this time. "I'm sorry."

Tori rested a hand on Jake's arm. "No need for apologies. I know you hate not being able to do what you're used to, but you can use this downtime for something good."

"I really need to be working." Jake scrubbed a hand over his face. "The farm needs me."

"Right now, you're not going to do the farm any good if you destroy what the surgeon repaired. Focus on healing. Let others step up and help."

"Why do you even care?"

Tori traced the edge of her iPad. "Because…that's what family does."

She was part of his family at one time.

She opened her Photos app and scrolled through the folders until she came across images taken by a friend that she'd been using for her fund-raiser research. She handed the tablet to Jake. "A friend of mine took these recently and thought they'd be a source of inspiration to help keep us focused. These heroes—they're struggling with a lot more than stitches."

With a scowl, he took it and sunk back into the cushions. He flipped through a few pictures of veterans with missing limbs, veterans going through therapy, veterans working with animals. All of their faces had been turned away from the camera. He flipped through a few more, then stopped. Using his thumb and index finger, he enlarged one of the photos and brought the tablet closer as his eyes narrowed. Then he sucked in a sharp breath. Color drained from his face, leaving his skin the color of the afghan that had fallen on the floor.

"What's wrong?"

"Where'd you say you got these photos?" He set the tablet aside, then scrubbed a shaky hand over his ashen face.

"A friend of mine took them. Why?"

"Where?"

"Some were taken at the VA hospital with permission. Others were taken at an animal shelter, then some were just candid shots."

"Call her. Find out." His clipped tones pierced her like carefully aimed verbal darts.

"What's going on?"

"Micah." He pointed at the screen.

"Your brother? What about him?"

"He's in one of those photos."

"Are you sure?"

"Of course I am." He dragged a hand through his hair, doing little to tame the wildness. "I'd recognize my own brother."

"But you can't see any of their faces."

Jake thrust out his left arm and turned it over. A tattoo of an oak tree with tangled roots inked his tanned skin. "Tuck, Evan, Micah and I got this matching tat after Mom was killed. There's a tree next to the farmhouse that remained unchanged when the tornado nearly wiped out everything else. Dad had said our family was like that tree—Holland strong and rooted deep to weather any storm." He picked up the iPad and handed it to her. "Check out this guy's arm."

Tori took the tablet and viewed the image of a bearded man with shaggy hair whose face was shadowed as he slept on a park bench wearing ripped jeans, worn combat boots and a ragged army sweatshirt pulled up to the elbow…exposing a tattoo identical to Jake's.

"We haven't heard from Micah in six months, not since he'd been medically discharged from the army after receiving service-related injuries. He cut all ties with us, and we've been trying to find him since. After one of Dad's friends shared about a farming program that teaches veterans how to farm so they can start their own businesses, Dad's been excited about offering something similar on Holland Hill. Since he can't do it alone, I offered to help—I lost a good friend who suffered from war-related injuries. If we can find Micah and bring him home, then maybe we can help him get back on his feet. Can you find out from your friend where this photo was taken? Maybe we can get a lead on what's been happening with him."

Color returned to Jake's face. His eyes lit as he took the tablet from her and looked at the photo again. The corner of his mouth turned up. For the first time since she'd arrived in town, Jake had something she hadn't seen in a long time.

Hope.

And this is what he wanted for his program—hope for those veterans who struggled with finding any in their situations.

The success of this fund-raiser weighed on her shoulders.

She could do this. She believed in her abilities.

She'd do what she could to help find more information about Jake's brother. Offer the missing piece in this family's puzzle.

Between that and the fund-raiser, maybe it would

be enough to prove to Jake that she had value and was worth having in his life...distraction or not. She needed to try...for both of their sakes.

Chapter Four

Tori had a new respect for farmers. Getting up at four thirty to be at the farm by 5:00 a.m...well, that bordered on ridiculous.

But she had given her word to help Jake and there was no way she was going back on it. Not with everything that was at stake.

She was more than the city slicker he'd pegged her as being. One worthy of a second chance.

She parked her car in the barnyard and headed toward the brightly lit milk house. Her brand-new rubber boots felt hot and clunky, but she couldn't exactly wear flip-flops to milk cows. She'd worn her oldest pair of jeans and threw a pink plaid button-down shirt on over a light pink T-shirt. Her hair had been pulled into a ponytail and looped through the back of her tan baseball cap. Good enough. No need to bother with makeup. The cows wouldn't care and Jake had made his lack of interest abundantly clear.

She opened the door to the milk house, the creak of the screen slicing through the predawn silence.

The steamy warmth enveloped her. A long cylindrical

milk tank sat off to her left as pipes and hoses snaked across the walls and ceiling. The opposite wall held a stainless steel deep sink, more pipes and a smaller clear tank. Two doors opened at the back of the milk house, one labeled Office and the other labeled Restroom.

A glance at the wall clock hanging between the two doors showed she was five minutes early, but Jake still beat her. One of the benefits of having a farm in the backyard. He stood on the step in front of a dingy swinging door.

She gave him a smile. "Good morning."

His eyes scanned her from head to toe. "Morning. Ready to get started?"

She nodded.

"I'll give you a quick overview first." He waved a hand over the room, then pointed to the overhead piping. "This is the milk house. Inside the barn, when the cows are milked, the milk travels into the milk receiver." He flattened his palm against a clear glass tank…kind of resembling a water cooler jug. "Once it's full, it pumps the milk through the overhead pipes to the bulk tank, where the milk is cooled quickly and kept until the milk truck arrives to pick it up."

Jake walked over to the deep sink and pointed to a rectangular box above it. "This is the vacuum pump control panel. This will remove air from the milking units and pipes in order to create a vacuum that is necessary to milk the cows. This button carries the milk into the receiving jar. This other button pushes water through the pipes and lines to clean and disinfect the milking system. Questions?"

So many. But where to start?

She shook her head, praying he wouldn't quiz her later. She'd need Divine Intervention to pass.

Jake returned to the swinging door and held it open. "Let's head into the milk barn and get started."

She brushed past him with the barest of touches— her shoulder against his arm—but it was enough to awaken her pulse.

Get a grip.

The pungent odor of manure caused her to gasp, then cough as her eyes watered. How did people get used to that smell?

She passed a series of metal bars, then followed Jake down four steps into a rectangular area lined with hoses.

He spread out his arms. "Welcome to the pit."

That's what it was called? Seriously?

"Before we get started, let me explain a few things." He waved his bandaged hand across the series of bars. "This is a parallel milking parlor, which allows us to milk eight cows at a time, and it offers cow comfort. Comfortable cows are better milk producers. These individual stalls allow them to eat their grain in peace and stand on warm rubber flooring that also helps to heat the room. Great in the winter."

Jake pressed a button, and gates on each side of the pit opened. Large cows lumbered into the stalls, eying her a moment before lowering their heads into the food troughs. Jake pulled out disposable gloves and handed them to her. "Put these on to protect your hands and to cut down on contamination."

He closed the gate, then lifted green and yellow cups off one of the bars. "This green cup is a predip solution we apply to the cows' udders before milking. It kills bacteria and cleans the teats. The yellow cup is the post-dip that conditions and protects the udders."

He moved to the first cow, applied the predip quickly and efficiently, then tore off a paper towel from the roll hanging on one of the bars. "Once we apply the predip, we grab a paper towel and wipe down the cow. The last thing we want is dirt and germs in the milk. Then we squirt milk from each teat to ensure there's no mastitis, an infection of the mammary glands." He wiped the cow again, tossed the used paper towel in the trash, then reached for a hose and sprayed away the squirted milk.

Jake picked up a weird-looking contraption that looked like an oversize claw and ran the back of his bandaged hand over the rubber ends. "This is a milker. These soft rubber liners do not hurt the cow. Once I turn on the vacuum, the milkers pulsate to mimic a calf feeding. They sense when the cow is finished and release automatically. Move the milkers out of the way and apply the postdip the same way as the predip. That cow leaves and another takes its place. Questions?"

Tori stared over Jake's shoulder at the cows and closed her eyes. How was she going to remember how to do everything?

"How do you know how much milk each cow produces?"

He pressed buttons on a control panel. "Our computer systems monitor each cow's output. They wear collars with computer chips in them, which feeds all the vital information into our computer systems."

"Seems like milking takes a long time."

He shrugged. "You get into a rhythm. We can milk eight cows at once, and it takes only a few minutes per cow."

"So then you're done after a couple of hours?"

Jake scoffed. "Maybe with the milking. After we're finished here, the equipment needs cleaned and sanitized, the stalls need to be hosed out, the barn needs to be cleaned and it's time to feed the calves. Once that's done, then we can head to the house for breakfast. Then out to the fields to plant, bale hay or harvest, depending on the season. Then we have milk inspectors, vet visits, paperwork and supplies to purchase."

"You do all of this by yourself?"

"Tuck does the evening milking before leaving for work. Dad takes care of the finances and the computer part of the business. I'm responsible for the morning milking and the bulk of the field work."

They'd only begun but his lowdown of a typical day wore her out already. "Well, I'm here now to lend a hand, so show me what to do."

"Shadow me for the first few cows, then you can do the other side."

Tori did as directed, then moved across the pit to the other cows, but the moment she touched the first cow's udders, the cow stepped back, startling her. She dropped the predip cup on the floor underneath the cow.

Oh, great. Now what?

Standing on her tiptoes and stretching as far as she could, Tori's fingers brushed the edge of the cup. The cow's leg came up and connected with her forearm, just barely missing her head.

"Victoria! What are you doing?" Jake hooked his left arm around her waist and pulled her back.

She rubbed her reddened, throbbing arm and quickly blinked back tears pooling in her eyes. "I dropped the cup and tried to get it."

"Next time ask for help. A cow's kick can cause serious damage."

"I'm sorry." She'd been saying that a lot lately.

"Don't sweat it." A muscle jumped in the side of his jaw, betraying his calm tone.

In her first five minutes, she proved to be more of a hindrance than a help, but she was determined to do better.

Jake grabbed the cup and hosed it off before handing it back to her. "Think you can handle the rest?"

Gritting her teeth against the growing pain in her arm, Tori nodded and returned to the cow.

She could do this.

For the next hour, Tori moved from cow to cow, but even with his bandaged hand, Jake moved quicker and more efficiently than she did with two good hands.

He was used to working alone. That was evident by the multiple times he turned and nearly tripped over her. But he didn't yell.

He didn't have to.

The deep sighing and flared nostrils spoke volumes.

Once the last cow returned to the barn, Tori wanted to curl up on the grimy floor and take a nap. Every muscle ached, including her black-and-blue arm. But the job wasn't done yet.

She headed out of the office with an armful of paper towels from the storage cabinet and headed back to the pit to refill the dispensers as Jake asked.

She pushed through the swinging door, and a strong spray of water hit her, soaking the front of her.

She yelped, threw her hands up to shield her face and dropped the rolls of towels, which bounced onto the floor. Her wet boot slipped on the edge of the slick step and she fell backward, her arms pinwheeling as she tried to grab something…anything…to break her fall.

Strong hands grabbed her arms as her back slammed into a chest.

"Oomph. For a little thing, you pack a punch."

Tori found her feet and twisted to find Tucker wearing a weary grin standing behind her. Dark spots dotted his blue uniform. She didn't even want to think about what they could be. She ran a shaky hand over her face. "Thanks for catching me. That fall would've been painful."

Jake pushed through the swinging door and jumped down the two steps. "Hey, are you okay?"

"I'm fine. Tucker caught me before I could fall."

"Thanks, bro."

"Looks like I came at the right time. You two are a dangerous combination."

In more ways than one.

Tori reclaimed the soggy paper towels and looked for a trash can. Not finding one, she hung on to them until Jake could direct her where to find one.

Jake pointed at Tucker's uniform. "Rough night?"

"Yeah. An accident. It was pretty bad."

"Sounds like you could use a hot shower and a comfortable bed."

"At this point, I'd take cold water and a cement pad if it meant I could close my eyes for a bit. But, hey, enough about me." He glanced at Tori and grinned. "You're off the hook, city girl."

Why did they keep calling her that?

"Hey, don't I get points for trying? And what am I off the hook for?"

"I talked to my supervisor and changed my hours so I can cover milking for you."

"You can't do that."

"Already did."

"And when are you going to sleep?"

"Sleep's overrated. Besides, I'm working daylights for the short term. I just need help with the kids."

"You got it." She'd take kids over cows any day of the week. Even though she knew about as much about both, at least kids could talk. "I'll help care for your kids. Annabeth will love having playmates. But I'd need to do it at the farmhouse." She looked at Jake. "Are you fine with that?"

He lifted a shoulder. "They're Tuck's kids. As long as he trusts you, that's all that matters."

"I understand that, but it would mean I'd be hanging around more. I didn't know if you…" Her voice trailed off as she bit her bottom lip and left the rest of her concern unspoken. He'd made it clear already how he felt about being around her.

She was a distraction.

But maybe this was one way she could help out without creating chaos.

Jake was going crazy already. He wasn't used to doing nothing around the farm. The rigid splint on his hand was a nuisance. Three more weeks and he could limit it to nighttime use.

Man, what a drag.

He couldn't afford the time away from his chores for the expected ten to twelve weeks. If he followed doctor's orders and did the recommended hand and finger exercises, then maybe he could resume light duty in six to eight weeks.

In the meantime, his family juggled their schedules to meet the demands of the farm while he wrangled a paintbrush.

Jake didn't know whether to hug Tucker or slug him when his brother changed his work schedule to take care of the milking. Sure, Jake kind of liked not being jarred awake by his alarm blaring at four in the morning, but then again, his body was so used to being up that early he was awake anyway. He'd been tempted to put on his barn clothes and give his brother a hand, but he stayed in bed enjoying the cool air circulating from the ceiling fan over his bed.

Even though he wouldn't have to work alongside Tori in the milk barn, there was plenty of work to be done at her house and on the fund-raiser.

And he was running out of time, especially while trying to do things one-handed.

Like painting the wall.

Trying to jockey the angled paintbrush with his left hand, Jake cut along the French door trim. Dove-gray paint smeared onto the white door frame.

He was making more of a mess than a preschooler during craft time.

Olivia and Landon could do a better job. Even Annabeth for that matter.

He set the brush across the top of the paint cup and reached for the damp rag to clean off the paint. He'd wanted to get the walls finished today so he could tackle the trim tomorrow, but with the lack of coordination using his left hand, he needed to admit defeat so he didn't create an even bigger mess.

"How's it going?"

Jake turned as the hardwood floor creaked beneath Tori's bare feet as she entered the room holding two glasses of iced tea and handed one to him. Poppy bounded in behind her and raced across the floor to sniff the paint tray. As if realizing no food was involved, she zipped out the door.

"Thanks." He shifted his eyes away from her light purple T-shirt and white shorts and drained half his glass, then glancing at his sloppy paint job, he shrugged. "Depends on your expectations, I guess. The kids could've done a better job. Although I'm sure you really wouldn't want Landon anywhere near that paint tray. He's got a knack for finding trouble."

Tori laughed, the sound bouncing through the empty room and pinging him in the chest. She shoved a hand in her front pocket and turned in circles in the middle of the room to survey his work.

Sunlight streamed in through the open window and hit her like a spotlight, turning her hair to white gold. A humid breeze stirred the stuffy air and tagged the loose strands around her face that had fallen from the knot on the top of her head.

She looked at him and smiled. "Actually I think you've done a bang-up job, especially with using only your left hand."

"My hand's not steady enough to cut around the trim."

"I can do it later. You can always help with the fundraiser if you want. Let's take a break. Annabeth's getting tired. Aunt Claudia offered to hang out at the farmhouse until your brother and dad return from his physical therapy appointment. That way the kids can take naps. Then we can head into town. I made a couple of appointments this afternoon to follow up with the letters I sent to local businesses outlining our objectives and asking them about becoming sponsors for the fund-raiser. You can turn on that country-boy charm and show your passion for the project. I'd like to swing by the printer and check on the presale tickets. And Aunt Claudia suggested a couple of caterers we could check out."

Which would be more challenging? Cramping his hand around a paintbrush for another couple of hours or spending alone time with Tori?

He'd been trying to keep his distance when possible, but even when she wasn't around, thoughts of her still crowded his head.

And that annoyed him.

But he couldn't be rude. After all, she was doing a great thing for his program. And his family.

Planning events was outside his wheelhouse, but if Tori was willing to step outside her comfort zone and help on the farm, then this was the least he could do. He needed to do whatever he could to help the project become a success.

Jake finished the rest of his tea and set the empty glass on the top step of the ladder positioned in front of the French doors that opened onto a small balcony that overlooked the backyard.

He bent to put the lid on the paint can. "I need to clean the brushes first."

"If you'd rather not go…"

Jake glanced over his shoulder to find Tori gnawing on the corner of her bottom lip. He hated the hesitation in her voice, especially knowing his attitude was the cause. "It's not that. I'm just...frustrated. We had an agreement, and I'm not holding up my end."

"It's not like you planned to cut your hand or need unexpected surgery."

"I should've worn gloves. It was a stupid mistake."

"Give yourself a break."

"I gave my word."

"And I appreciate that, but this was beyond your control. Besides, you've managed to paint two rooms with your left hand."

"Where are the kids?" Jake grabbed the paint tray with the used brushes.

Tori reached for his empty glass. "Playing with Play-Doh on the floor in the kitchen."

He shot her a grin as they left the room and headed for the stairs. "You're a brave woman."

"They can't hurt anything, and it cleans up quickly."

Jake followed her down the steps, keeping his eyes on his feet rather than the appealing image in front of him, and headed for the kitchen. "Hey, guys. What are you making?"

After setting the paint tray in the sink, Jake dropped to his haunches in front of the flowered plastic table-cloth and took a small ball of Play-Doh Olivia handed him. He rolled it between his fingers as Olivia, Landon and Annabeth played with blue, green and yellow Play-Doh. A rainbow of cookie cutter shapes, small rolling pins and plastic scissors lay scattered around them.

"Uncle Jake, check out my snake." Landon held up a green lumpy-looking snake.

"Great job, buddy."

"I'm making a unicorn." Olivia added stumpy blue

legs to a blob of Play-Doh with what must have been the unicorn's horn sticking out of the animal's forehead.

Jake cupped his niece's cheek. "Looks great, Liv." He turned to Annabeth. "What are you making, little one?"

Annabeth shot him a shy smile, then dropped her chin. She picked up her yellow ball and added a smaller ball on top. "Piggy."

"Did you have fun seeing the piggies again the other day?"

Still smiling, she nodded, then returned her attention to the blob of dough in her chubby little hands.

Jake straightened and looked at Tori. "I can't believe you managed to keep them corralled so well."

"Play-Doh is magical. Kids love it."

"You're really good with them."

She shrugged. "I've had very little experience around kids, but I've always wanted a big family. I took a couple of child development classes as electives in college."

Jake moved to the sink and ran water into the paint tray. She joined him and added a squirt of dish soap.

"We could've had that, you know."

Had he voiced that thought out loud?

He shot a glance at her to see pink coloring her cheeks. Apparently he had. But it wasn't like he could take it back. Might as well push in deeper with the one question that'd been weighing on him for years.

He took a deep breath and rinsed the brushes under running water, spraying paint against the sides of the stainless steel sink. He shut off the water a little more forcefully than necessary and turned to her, keeping his voice low. "Why, Tori? That's all I want to know."

She didn't pretend not to know what he was talking about. She glanced at the kids, then looked at him with an expression that sent a shiver across his skin. "You want to get into this now? Right here? It's not really the best place or time."

"It's never the right time."

She gritted her teeth, then gripped the edge of the sink. "I had no choice, Jake. I did it to protect you."

"Of course you had a choice—you're a grown woman. You chose to end our marriage—"

"Daddy!" Livie's cries jerked Jake's attention away from Tori's ashen face to the doorway, where his dad and brother stood, their eyes narrowed and directed at him.

Perfect.

Even though Jake had kept his voice down, he had no doubt they'd heard his response to Tori.

Tori left him at the sink, reached for a towel, then crossed the room to talk to his dad and Tuck. Liv and Landon wrapped their arms around Tuck's legs. Jake turned around and flipped the water back on.

Dad crossed the room to stand next to him and scraped a weathered hand across the top of his graying brush cut. Deep lines edged the corners of his eyes as his lips turned up in a half smile. He clamped a hand on Jake's shoulder and spoke low so only Jake could hear his words. "Sounds like there's something we need to talk about."

Without replying, Jake scrubbed the paint from the brushes. The quicker he cleaned up his mess, the better for everyone.

Chapter Five

The conversation Jake had been dreading all day was about to happen. No more dodging the truth. But the last thing Jake wanted was to disappoint his dad. Again. No matter how he answered the question, he'd have to deal with some sort of disapproval.

He speared a green bean and poked his fork into one of the remaining bites of meat loaf on his plate.

"Jake? Did you hear me?"

"Yeah, I did." Jake hunched over his plate.

"Planning to answer anytime tonight?"

He glanced at Dad. "Why's that important?"

Dad reached for his iced tea and sighed. "It's not, I guess. None of my business, but you're my son, and I'm concerned. From the moment I saw you two together, something seemed off. And after Claudia mentioned you'd known Tori while you were in the service...well, I couldn't help but wonder. Are you and Tori married?"

Jake set his fork on his plate and shoved it aside, his appetite gone. Reaching for his empty glass, he stood and walked to the sink to refill it. He stared out the window and searched his brain for the right words as he downed the cool liquid. He faced Dad and Tuck, who'd also stopped eating and watched him. "My relationship with Tori is...complicated."

"How so?"

"I didn't know she was Claudia's niece until she arrived in Shelby Lake. Tori and I met one night at the NCO club on base when she spilled a tray of drinks on me. We started dating." Jake paused and rubbed a thumb and forefinger over his tired eyes. "She'd just graduated college and was spending the summer with her sister, who had been stationed there with her husband. Kendra is now serving overseas."

"Right. Claudia mentioned that. She's divorced?"

"Not sure. Tori mentioned her brother-in-law had walked out after Annabeth's first birthday."

"Tori's a good sister and aunt to step in to care for that little girl."

"Yes, she is." Jake had to give her that.

"So then what happened?"

The quicker he said it, the sooner they could end this conversation.

"We eloped, but our marriage didn't last long. She's now my ex-wife. So there you have it."

"Whoa." Tucker, who'd been slouching in his chair, straightened and shot a look at Jake. "Dude, that's rough."

No kidding.

Dad looked down at his folded hands resting on the table.

The ticking of the second hand on the clock above the sink competed with the occasional drip from the faucet as the only sounds in the usually noisy room.

The silence spoke louder than yelling.

And that was why he'd kept his relationship with Tori to himself all those years.

Jake scrubbed a hand over his face. Not wanting to see Dad's disappointment, Jake turned around and started rinsing the dinner dishes and loading them in the dishwasher.

"Did you divorce her?"

Jake shut off the water and reached for a dish towel. "What? No way. I love… I loved her. Three weeks into my deployment, divorce papers were delivered through my CO. I was blindsided. I tried to contact her, but she refused to speak to me."

"Was that why you took emergency leave to return stateside?"

"Partly. I wanted to track her down and figure out what had gone wrong. But the night I got the papers, I was supposed to stand duty. My buddy Leo offered to cover for me, and I let him. He was out on patrol and ran over an IED, causing him to lose his leg. It should've been me that night. Then while home, the tornado hit. We lost Mom, and suddenly my divorce was the last thing on my mind."

Dad struggled to his feet, wincing as he pressed a hand to his lower back. He shuffled over to Jake and cupped his hands over his shoulders. "Son, you've had a rough handful of years."

Jake looked into his father's eyes, the same shade as his own. Instead of anger and disapproval, Dad's tanned face that spoke of years in the outdoors and raising four boys softened. His eyes shadowed with compassion, which caused a sudden knot to twist Jake's throat.

Wetness dampened his eyes, and he blinked rapidly to hold back the pressure.

"I wish you would've told us. That's too heavy of a burden to carry by yourself."

"It was a foolish, reckless mistake that resulted in devastating consequences. It was my fault, my responsibility. My burden to bear."

"Not true. We're a family—we share the burdens. And God invites us to come to him with our burdens. He promises to give us rest."

"Easier said than done, Pops. Besides, after the tornado nearly destroyed the farm and our family, I had bigger problems to deal with."

"Even when we think something's impossible, everything is possible with God. Claim His promises in faith."

Faith.

He had that once.

Faith in God. Faith in family. Faith in relationships.

But that was before life betrayed him and buckled his knees.

Dad let go of his shoulders and pulled Jake into a hug, wrapping his arms tightly around his stiff body.

For a moment, Jake felt like a kid again. When he'd had a problem, he'd always gone running to his dad because he'd always have a solution.

When did he stop running to his father? His Heavenly Father?

When did he decide he needed to find his own solutions?

The night Dad's tough love changed Jake's life. The night when his own stupidity and reckless choice of underage drinking to impress a girl got him arrested and landed him in jail, causing him to lose his college scholarship. When Dad reminded him he needed to find a solution to his problem. And the next day he'd enlisted in the Marine Corps.

Closing his eyes, he drew in the strength from Dad's muscular arms. Maybe, just maybe, he could hold on to some of that strength for those days when he didn't feel so strong, when he didn't have the solutions. Only problems.

Second to his granddad, Dad was the wisest man Jake knew. He'd always admired his ability to hold on to his faith even after grieving the loss of his wife, multiple surgeries to repair the damage to his back and needing to rebuild the farm passed down to him by his father.

Dad released him and clapped him on the back. "It's not too late, you know."

"What isn't?"

"Another chance with Tori. If you still love her, fight for her. Her showing up at Holland Hill could be God offering the two of you a second chance. Question is, are you willing to step out in faith to take it?"

At one time he'd vowed before God to love, honor and cherish her, but that love had been eaten away by heartache and his own failure to make his wife happy.

"And when it doesn't work out? Then what?"

"Life doesn't promise guarantees, Jake. And you can't stop taking risks to prevent the hurts from happening. Give her a reason to stay." Dad took the dish towel from him and flung it over his shoulder. "We're Holland strong, remember? We may bend, but we can't be broken. Given the junk we've gone through in the past five years, that's saying a lot. Let me finish these dishes. I've been sitting too long today and my bones are stiff."

Needing some fresh air, Jake headed for the screen door. He stepped outside to find Tucker stretched out on one of the wooden deck chairs, his eyes closed and his hands tucked behind his neck. "He's right, you know."

"Who?" Jake knew the answer, but asking the question gave him a second more time to brace himself for the knowledge his younger brother wanted to drop on him.

"Dad." Tucker sat up and flung his legs over the side of the chair, bracing his elbows on his knees. He twisted the wedding ring he still wore two years after his wife's tragic death due to a food allergy. "Life doesn't promise a guarantee. Or a happily-ever-after. I mean, we thought Mom and Dad were going to be together forever. Then Mom was killed. I never expected to be a widower in my twenties trying to raise two babies on my own. Life stinks at times, bro. No denying that. I'm sorry to hear what happened between you and Tori. But she's here now. Man, if I had a second chance with Rayne, I'd be all over that. If you want a second chance with Tori, fight for her because you never know how long you're going to have together. Don't waste a minute of it."

A moment later, the screen door slammed behind Tucker as he returned inside, leaving Jake staring up at the dusky sky. Strokes of rusty orange faded into the palest shades of pink as the navy sky hovered, waiting to light the earth with its multitude of stars. Around him the night noises sang their choruses as bullfrogs croaked and peepers chirped. Tucker's advice echoed inside Jake's head. He wrestled with untangling the wisdom and the emotions he'd stored away for so long because dealing with them was just too painful.

Maybe it was time to give Tori another chance.

But what if he wasn't enough?

What if she left again?

Give her a reason to stay.

Dad's words swirled through his thoughts, but his own insecurities wondered if he was truly strong enough to make that happen.

This impromptu pizza party had to go well. Had to. Her reputation was at stake. She needed to show Jake she'd moved beyond burning toast and frozen dinners. But being in the Holland kitchen with him made Tori nervous.

And on Father's Day.

But Jake assured her it wouldn't be a problem.

After two weeks of painting rooms and completing the last one today, she'd suggested celebrating with pizza, expecting him to decline.

But, to her surprise, he agreed.

Once she offered to make it from scratch, Jake had teased her, saying opening a box of Chef Boyardee didn't count as a recipe.

Proving it, however, was problematic once she realized nothing had been moved into the newly painted kitchen. Uncertain of Claudia's plans, the last thing Tori wanted to be was an imposition.

On anyone.

But Jake had solved it by suggesting they make the pizzas at the farmhouse as long as she didn't mind extra mouths.

The more the merrier. And she meant it. She loved the noise and chaos of family. Especially his family.

The farmhouse kitchen with white subway tile back-splash, white shaker cabinets and reclaimed barn board countertops invited family to hang out and laugh while they cooked and ate together. A weathered plank with

Give Us This Day Our Daily Bread hung over the rectangular table edged against the window that looked
over the side yard.

Jake had mentioned how they'd given his mother the
kitchen of her dreams, but she didn't live long enough
to enjoy it. And the table had belonged to Jake's great-
grandparents.

So much history...so much family in one room.

If anyone had told her a month ago...or even a week
ago...she'd be standing in the Holland kitchen, she
wouldn't have believed it.

But here she was kneading dough and making pizza
with Jake.

And she still couldn't wrap her mind around it.

Tori turned the dough, folded it, kneaded it one last
time and placed it in the oiled glass bowl. After covering it with a blue dish towel, she set it on the back of the
stove. She reached for the red-stained wooden spoon
and stirred the simmering sauce. The tangy scents of
the tomatoes tangled with the minced garlic, fresh oreg-
ano and basil. She set the spoon back on the rest and
reduced the heat under the pot.

She rinsed out a worn knitted dishrag and wiped up
the flour off the table, careful not to spill any on the
plank flooring. She rinsed it out again, then draped it
over the edge of the deep single-bowl farmhouse sink,
and then washed her hands, drying them on the red-
checked apron Jake had loaned her.

A peek at the dough showed it was starting to rise.
She gave the sauce another stir, covered the pot, then
turned off the heat.

Tori pushed through the screen door to step onto the

shaded back deck, where Chuck and Jake stretched out on wooden deck chairs while drinking iced tea.

Annabeth raced barefoot across the grass after Livie and Landon, their high-pitched screams and giggles echoing across the hilltop and drowning out the country music station playing softly in the kitchen.

Tori folded her arms in front of her and drew in a deep breath.

Content.

That's how she felt.

For the moment.

And for the first time in quite a while.

But for tonight, she'd cling to it, hold it close and savor it because experience reminded her it wouldn't last.

Don't borrow trouble.

Her sister's advice from their last Skype chat rang in her ears.

"Those are some good smells coming from the kitchen."

Tori looked down at Chuck to find him smiling at her. He raised his glass of tea and winked.

"You're probably smelling the pizza sauce. Jake made it, so he gets the credit."

"I made it using your recipe." Eyes closed, his words laced with a hint of humor threaded through her, seaming those ragged edges around her heart. His white untucked button-down shirt opened at the throat with sleeves rolled to his elbow emphasized his tan skin.

"And not a single can was opened…huh, imagine that."

He opened one eye and peered at her. "We haven't eaten it yet. I have Pizza Pete's on speed dial."

Another time she would've leaned over and given him a playful kiss in response to his teasing. Tonight, though, she simply took a mental photo of the look on his face, storing it in one of the deep pockets in her memory. For once she wasn't taxing his patience.

As Jake turned to respond to something his dad had asked, Tori's eyes roamed over his face. The deep lines around his eyes and mouth had softened. The furrowed brows smoothed out as laughter lit up his eyes.

Oh, how she longed to run her hands through his hair or draw a finger over the angles of his jaw before tracing his lips and covering them with her own.

She longed for a lot of things.

She released a sigh as a sudden cloud of melancholy descended over her, chilling her flesh. She rubbed her bare arms to warm her skin.

Think happy thoughts.

That's what she told Annabeth when her niece grew sad over missing her mommy.

Turning, Tori reached for the screen doorknob just as a scream split the air. She jerked around to find Annabeth facedown in the grass.

Jake shot out of the chair, jumped the three deck steps and raced over to her, scooping her in his arms. Tori hurried behind him.

Blood gushed from her nose and mouth, soaking the front of Jake's shirt.

Tori reached for her, but Jake nodded to the house. "Grab the door for me. Let's get her inside."

Rushing up the deck stairs, Tori jerked the screen door open as Jake carried Annabeth into the kitchen. He sat the crying child on the counter next to the sink, then opened one of the drawers and pulled out a clean dish towel. He soaked it under cold running water and squeezed it out one-handed.

Tori wrapped an arm around Annabeth, holding her close. She brushed tangled hair away from her face as Jake gently wiped away blood that continued to stream from her nose.

He grabbed a wad of paper towels, wet them and thrust them at Tori. "See if she'll let you pinch her nose closed. Don't lean her back. I'm going to wake up Tucker."

Tori grabbed Jake's arm. "Oh, no. Don't do that. We can handle a bloody nose."

Jake shook his head, shot a look at Annabeth, then back to her. Without a word, he opened his hand to show Tori part of a small pearly tooth.

Tori's eyes widened and she swallowed her alarm so she didn't upset her niece even more. Nodding to Jake, Tori picked up Annabeth, carried her to the table and sat with the child on her lap. She cradled her close and pressed the paper towels to Annabeth's face as she pinched her nose gently.

Annabeth jerked her head from side to side, trying to move away from Tori's hand. Tears streamed down her grubby face and pooled in the creases in her neck.

"Sweetie, you have to sit still and let Auntie Tori help fix your boo-boo."

"Hurts." She pointed to her mouth.

"I know, honey. But the sooner we get your nose to stop bleeding, the sooner the owies will stop hurting."

Heavy footsteps thundered on the staircase. A second later, Jake reappeared in the kitchen with Tucker on his heels. Dressed in a T-shirt and nylon basketball shorts,

Tucker scrubbed a hand over his face, stifling a yawn, and pushed past Jake to kneel in front of Annabeth.

He set a black bag on the floor next to Tori's feet and unzipped it, pulling out a stuffed tan bear. "Hey, punkin. What's going on?"

"I falled."

He pulled on a pair of blue rubber gloves, then brushed hair off her face and rubbed a thumb across her cheek. "You poor thing. Can I take a look in your mouth?" He held up the bear. "This is my friend Pickles. You want to hold him for me?"

Annabeth nodded and clutched the bear to her chest as Tori removed the paper towels so Tucker could shine his light into Annabeth's mouth. She coughed and choked, then vomited in Tori's lap, which caused the child to wail again.

Tori's eyes watered as she pressed her cheek to the top of Annabeth's head. "Shh, it's going to be okay, honey. I promise."

Jake moved behind Tori and untied her apron strings, then reached under Annabeth to remove the soiled fabric to the sink. She shot him a smile of thanks.

"Jake, grab me some wet towels."

Jake did as his brother instructed and handed them to Tucker.

"Tori, hold her still but keep her head up."

Tori turned Annabeth so she could cradle her niece's small frame in the crook of her arm but kept her head upright and braced against her shoulder.

Tucker touched the child's upper gums, causing Annabeth to cry out and grab at his hands. "I'm sorry, punkin. I'm almost done."

Tori's heart twisted as she tried to calm the sobbing

child. She turned her head as tears filled her own eyes and connected with Jake, who watched them with such a look of tenderness that Tori's heart caved even deeper in her chest. He strode over to the table and rested a hand on her shoulder, giving her a gentle squeeze. The weight of his touch funneled strength through her. She brushed a cheek across his hand, then returned her focus to Annabeth.

Jake moved his hand across her upper back and settled it behind her neck, kneading her tense muscles gently.

Tucker glanced at Jake, then at Tori. "Does Annabeth have any allergies?"

Tori shook her head. "Not that we're aware of."

"I'll give her some children's ibuprofen to help with the pain." He pulled out a bottle of orange-colored medicine and shook it. He extracted a small amount with a plastic syringe and poised it in front of Annabeth and touched her chin. "Hey, sweetie, can you open your mouth for me again? I want to give you some medicine that will help you feel better."

Annabeth opened her mouth wide enough for Tucker to dispense the liquid along her inner cheek, then she turned her face into Tori's shoulder, smearing a dribble of medicine on her shirt. As Annabeth's tears subsided, a shudder racked her small body.

Tori tightened her hold and rocked the child, who kept Pickles in her clutches.

Tucker gathered the soggy, stained towels and used paper towels and carried everything to the trash. He pulled off his gloves, tossing them, then headed to the sink to scrub his hands. "A child's nose is small with lots of arteries. I'm sure she's going to be fine. As far as her tooth goes, Jake rinsed it and put it in a glass of milk, but since it's a baby tooth, it may not be worth trying to put back in her mouth. She needs to see a pediatric dentist because her gums are swelling. I suggest calling first thing in the morning. If she has another bloody nose or if her mouth begins to bleed, take her to the emergency department at the hospital."

"Thanks so much." Tori's gaze shifted between the brothers standing side by side in front of the sink, then lingered a second longer on Jake. "Both of you. I'm sorry for pulling you out of bed, Tucker. Jake mentioned you got called in to cover a shift tonight."

He waved away her apology. "Don't be sorry. I was half-awake anyway. Great smells drifted up the steps."

Tori shot a horrified look at the stove.

The pizza.

She shifted Annabeth in her arms, then stood and picked up one corner of the dish towel covering the bowl to see dough had risen above the rim.

Her shoulders sagged. It looked perfect.

But she was in no condition to cook.

She glanced at her blood-soaked T-shirt and soiled clothes, shot a look at Jake, and shrugged. "Looks like you may have to call Pizza Pete's after all. I need to take Annabeth home, give her a bath and put her to bed."

So much for impressing him with her culinary skills.

Jake pressed his back against the counter. "Bathe her here. I'm sure Livie has jammies she can wear. I'll loan you one of my shirts. Dad and I can get the pizzas in the oven. You need to eat."

"Did I hear my name?" The screen door slammed as Chuck walked into the kitchen holding hands with grubby Olivia and Landon.

Jake repeated his conversation with Tori.

Chuck looked down at his grandkids. "Wanna help Grandpa make some pizzas?"

"Yes." They spoke in unison.

"Better get washed up, then." Chuck guided them to the sink, pulling out a step stool for them to stand on.

As water splashed in the sink, Jake placed a hand on the small of Tori's back and guided her and Annabeth out of the kitchen.

Once again, Jake to the rescue.

Tori had been taking care of herself for so long that it felt good once in a while to lean on someone else. But if this continued, he was going to think she was more trouble than she was worth and head in the opposite direction. And that was the last thing she wanted.

She needed to do a better job of taking care of her own problems and less relying on Jake. Especially if he didn't want to be a part of her future.

Chapter Six

Tori had no business being in the kitchen as Jake, Tucker, Chuck and Aunt Claudia laughed together while they assembled and baked the pizzas with Olivia and Landon. Pretending to be a part of a family that wasn't hers.

No, she was the outsider…the interloper. The one who didn't belong.

Should she walk in? Or head back to the living room and hang out in case Annabeth woke up?

She should've taken Annabeth back to Claudia's to bathe her and put her to bed as she originally intended. But the longing to be a part of the activity caused her to give in to Jake's suggestion of bathing her niece at the farmhouse.

Now that Annabeth was curled up on the couch in the living room and sound asleep, Tori stood in the doorway biting her bottom lip as her fingers dug into the cuffs of Jake's borrowed sweatshirt, which hung past her hips, but she didn't care. She'd washed up quickly while Annabeth played in the bubbles Jake had thought to add to her water.

She needed to let her sister know about Annabeth, but because of the six-hour time difference between them, she didn't see the sense in waking her in the middle of the night.

A popular country song came on the radio, and Tucker turned up the volume. He reached for Olivia's small hands and danced with her in the middle of the room. Her giggles were even sweeter than the music when he picked her up in his arms and twirled her across their pretend dance floor. Landon stood on a chair next to Jake and counted as he placed pepperoni on one of the pizzas.

Chuck washed up their prep dishes while Claudia tore lettuce for a salad.

This was what being a part of a family was about—everyone working together to make things happen.

Not working hard to please and never feeling like she didn't measure up. No stony silences across from the dinner table when she said the wrong thing. Not standing alone during graduation while other families laughed and hugged and took pictures together.

Chuck caught her eye and straightened, reaching for a dish towel. He dried his hands, then tossed it on the counter and wandered over to her, his constant smile in place. "Where's AB?"

Tori jerked a thumb over her shoulder. "She's sleeping on the couch in the family room. I hope it's okay."

"Of course. If she wakes up, she'll be able to hear us. This rowdy crew doesn't seem to be dying down anytime soon." Chuck leaned a shoulder against the door frame and crossed his arms over his chest.

"You have a great family."

Chuck turned and eyed his crew with pride. "Yes, I

do. And I don't forget it for a minute." He nodded toward Jake and Tucker. "They've been through a lot, but they're strong."

Tori had no doubts about that. The strength this family had shown through adversity humbled her. After seeing the hope in Jake's eyes once he saw Micah's photo, she wanted to do what she could to bring this family back together. Claudia had given her Evan's phone number, and although she'd gotten his voice mail, she left a message and hoped he'd reach out to her. Jake had said Evan and Micah were pretty tight, so maybe Evan would know how to get in touch with Micah. But that had been several days ago. And wouldn't Evan share Micah's whereabouts with the family if he knew where his brother was? Still, it didn't hurt to ask.

A timer dinged.

"Duty calls." Chuck retrieved a quilted blue pot holder and opened the oven to pull out two steaming pizzas—one covered in cheese and pepperoni and the other with ham and pineapple. "Hey, Landon, is that pizza ready to go in the oven?"

"Yep." He jumped off the chair and reached for the metal pan on the counter, holding it steady in both hands. As he turned, the pan tilted sideways and would've slid if Jake hadn't been quick to right it. Uncle Jake to the rescue. Again.

The man was great at being in the right place at the right time.

Their eyes tangled, and for a moment, she couldn't move. Couldn't breathe. The laughter and music faded into the background as Jake crossed the room to stand in front of her close enough for her to feel the heat radiating from him in the warm kitchen. He nodded to the stove. "Grab some pizza while it's hot. Even if it's been ruined with fruit."

She smiled and lowered her voice. "You remembered."

Her breath hitched in her chest as he reached up and ran two fingers through the hair around her face, then held up a small leaf.

Of course.

He was being kind getting something from her hair... probably left from Annabeth. And she was ridiculous, reading something into his touch that wasn't there.

She took the leaf, crushing it in her palm. "Thanks."

He touched her chin, lifting her face to look at her. His softened expression turned Tori's bones to jelly. "There's very little I've forgotten, Victoria."

Instead of the censure that usually came with her given name, his tone spoke of tenderness, filling her with something she was almost too afraid to claim... hope. Was there hope for her and Jake?

That thought stayed with her ten minutes later as she took her pizza and glass of iced tea out to the back deck. She sat in one of the Adirondack chairs, set her plate on the side table and drew her knees to her chest. She brushed her cheek against the softness of Jake's sweatshirt, inhaling the scent of fabric softener. She rolled her shoulders to try to loosen the tight muscles from painting all day. She picked up her pizza and sank her teeth into the ham and pineapple, appreciating the tangy sweetness.

She didn't care how much the guys ribbed her about her favorite toppings, claiming fruit didn't belong with meat. She was touched Jake had remembered because she hadn't mentioned it.

As she chewed, she rested her head against the back of the chair and looked at the stars, thinking back over Jake's gentleness and the way he helped with Annabeth. And the tenderness of his touch as he rubbed Tori's neck.

If only things had been different. If only she hadn't been such a fool.

The screen door banged, startling Tori and jerking her upright. Chuck stepped onto the deck with a pizza pan in one hand and a spatula in the other. "Hey…oh, sorry. I didn't mean to scare you. Was just checking to see if you were ready for another slice yet."

"Thanks, but I've barely touched this one." She held up the partially eaten slice.

"No worries. Plenty more when you're ready." He turned to go.

"Hey, Chuck?" Tori set her pizza on her plate and brushed her hands together.

"Yeah?"

"Thanks. For everything. For allowing me to barge in and be a part of it. Especially with it being Father's Day and all."

"Young lady, you are welcome here anytime. I mean that." With the motion light shining behind him and the moonlight overhead, Tori couldn't make out his expression, but the warmth in his tone loosened the knots in her stomach.

Chuck headed back to the kitchen, but a moment later he stepped back onto the deck, his hands full of his own food. "Mind if I join you?"

"Of course not."

He settled into what seemed to be his favorite chair. He turned his plate in his hand, then set it on the floor next to his feet. He leaned forward and rested his elbows on his knees, clasping his hands in front of him. "Jake told us about your past with him."

Heat prickled her neck and crawled up her face. She dropped her gaze to her half-finished pizza, her appetite vanishing. "I'm so sorry."

"For what?"

She shrugged, searching for the right words. "Hurting your son?"

"I appreciate that. A parent hates seeing his kid in pain. I don't know what all he's told you, but the past few years have been hard on Jake. He's suffered a lot of loss. If you don't mind an old man's advice—be patient with him. He returned home from the service a changed man. He's as stubborn as a mule, but he's fiercely loyal to those he loves."

She nodded. "I know." The weight of Chuck's words burdened her, especially knowing her cowardly actions were part of the reason for Jake's changes. "You're a good dad. He's fortunate to have you. Not everyone's been as blessed as Jake and Tucker."

"Speaking from experience?"

Tori hesitated, then nodded slowly. "My mom died while giving birth to me. And I don't think my father ever forgave me for that."

"I'm sorry."

She gave him a wry smile. "Thanks."

"Did you get along with your dad?"

"On the surface. My father had high standards, and I spent most of my childhood failing to please him. I think my sister joined the military to escape his control."

"That's a tough way to grow up. A child shouldn't have to wonder if her father truly loves her. Mind if I ask a personal question?"

"Sure."

Chuck cleared his throat. "Are you a Christian, Tori?"

She nodded, almost relieved it was about something she had confidence in. "Yes, I am."

"Then you know you have a Heavenly Father who loves you without condition. To Him, you are His favorite one." Chuck reached for her hand and gave it a gentle squeeze.

Tori blinked back the rush of tears and tried to swallow past the lump in her throat. "I do know that. But…"

"But what?"

"Even though I know in my heart that God loves me, my head gets in the way with a lot of self-doubt. The Bible tells us there's nothing we can do to earn God's love, yet I struggle with measuring up…with being good enough…with being deserving of His love."

"But that's the awesome thing about God's grace. None of us deserves it. Yet, He gives it freely, without condition because of His overwhelming love for us. There are many things you can doubt in life, Tori, but God's love isn't one of them."

Still holding on to her hand, Chuck stood, then pulled her to her feet. He wrapped his arms around her. "I don't know what happened between you and Jake, but something tells me your marriage didn't end because you stopped loving him. God has amazing ways of untangling our troubles if we're willing to let Him. He can redeem broken families."

Tears slid silently down Tori's face as she rested her cheek on his shoulder. He murmured words over her, and she realized he was praying. For her. A sob shuddered in her chest, and Chuck tightened his grip.

When was the last time anyone had prayed for her?

Chuck reached over and grabbed Tori's napkin out from under her plate. He handed it to her, then tipped up her chin. "God loves you. Remember that. Stop trying so hard to please other people, including my son. You have amazing gifts, and I'm grateful for the way you're using them to help my family."

"Thank you, Chuck." Tori wadded the soggy napkin in her fist, then lifted watery eyes to him. "I wish my dad had been more like you. I'm sorry to be so emotional. It's my first Father's Day without him, and even though we had a difficult relationship, he was...well, he was still my dad."

Chuck pressed a kiss to her forehead. "I'm sorry for your loss. My dad's been gone over a decade, but a day doesn't pass without me missing him. Something tells me we're going to be seeing a lot of each other, sweetheart. I'm just down the road, and I could always use another friend. Anytime you want to talk, I'm willing to listen."

Another father could have given her a cold shoulder for the way she treated his son.

But not Chuck.

No, he was a rare one who showed love without condition. Something she wasn't used to having, but a gift she wouldn't take for granted.

But if things with Jake didn't work out, she wouldn't lose only the man she loved, but the family she wanted to claim as her own.

Jake glanced at his watch. Despite being benched from farming the past few weeks because of his bum hand, he still managed to finish milking in record time.

And without anyone else's help.

Maybe he could talk to the doctor about releasing him early as long as he promised to take it easy.

But was that a promise he'd be able to keep?

No need to worry about that right now.

He wanted to grab a quick shower and another cup of coffee and head into town to check on Annabeth.

And Tori.

Jake didn't mean to eavesdrop, but overhearing his dad's conversation with her last night made him realize just how different his childhood was from Tori's. She hadn't talked much about her father while they were married, and he hadn't pried because it caused her pain. And the last thing he wanted was to hurt his wife.

Wife.

It seemed like forever ago instead of only six years.

In the month she'd been in Shelby Lake, he caught glimpses of the Tori he'd fallen in love with, but she'd also changed. She wore a veil of vulnerability as fragile as an eggshell. She appeared strong, but he was afraid that after one too many cracks, she'd be broken beyond repair.

He didn't want to be the cause of that pain.

But he wasn't ready yet to jump in with both feet.

He'd done that once and still bore the scars.

Maybe it was time to let go of the hurt that kept him at a distance.

The milk house door slammed behind him as he cut through the backyard for the farmhouse. Claudia's cherry-red SUV was parked in the driveway.

A little early for a visit.

Hopefully everything was okay.

Maybe something happened with Annabeth during the night.

Or Tori…

Jake picked up his pace, took the deck steps in one stride, toed off his boots and stepped into the kitchen. Finding it empty, he followed the sounds of low voices and a soft giggle. He reached the living room and—

Whoa!

He spun on his heel and retreated soundlessly for the back deck, where he thrust his feet back into his boots and hurried down the steps.

His gut twisted. Despite the early morning rising temperature, a cold sweat slicked his skin. He cut across the grass and headed for the road.

Dad and Claudia?

Kissing?

When did that happen? Why hadn't Dad said anything? Why hide it?

Questions thrummed inside his head as Jake walked past the pasture where cows grazed lazily in the morning sunshine and the even rows of ankle-high cornstalks studded the fields. Movement out of the corner of his eye drew his attention away from his dad's hidden romance to find he'd walked toward Tori's house.

"Jake." Annabeth ran across the yard and barreled into his legs, wrapping her arms around his knees. She jerked back, pinched her nose and wrinkled her face. "Pee-eww. You stinky."

Jake laughed, reached down and swung her up into his arms. "Hey, little one. How are you feeling?"

"My mouth hurted." She opened her mouth and pointed to her upper jaw still red and swollen. "I broked a tooth."

"You sure did. Does it still hurt?"

"Nuh-uh. Aunt Tori gaved me orange medicine."

He gave her a quick squeeze, then put her down. No sense in ruining her pink T-shirt and polka-dotted denim overalls with his barn smell. She ran across the yard to the porch, where she picked up Pickles, the tan bear Tucker had given her.

Tori knelt in the front of the flower bed rimming the front and side of the porch. A flat of pink petunias, yellow and purple pansies, and some other blue flower he didn't recognize sat next to her. "Good morning. What brings you down the road so early?" She pushed her sunglasses on her head and eyed his faded T-shirt and worn jeans, then scowled. "And why are you in barn clothes? The doctor hasn't released you yet."

"Tucker got called in to cover a shift, remember? Dad can't stand that long yet to milk, so I had to do it. I wore a glove to cover the stitches and used my hand as little as possible."

It was kind of nice having someone show concern for his well-being. "What are you guys doing up so early? After AB's tumble last night, I figured she'd still be asleep."

Tori glanced at her niece digging in the dirt with a small pink shovel. "Hardly. Very little keeps her down. She was wide awake at six, so Aunt Claudia and I decided to check out a greenhouse plant sale. I found these annuals and decided to add some color to the flower beds. We have an appointment with a pediatric dentist in an hour—I'm concerned about the swelling around her gums." Tori reached for one of the packs of flowers and pried a plant loose from the plastic tray. She set it in the hole and covered it with dirt, her ponytail falling in front of her as she leaned forward. "You haven't answered my question."

"Which one?"

"What are you doing down at this end of the road?" She turned and gestured toward the house. "We're done painting. The roofers will be done by the end of the week. You're no longer obligated to be here." Tori sat back on her heels and brushed a gloved hand across her forehead, leaving a smudge of dirt on her skin.

"I could leave if you'd like."

"That's not what I meant."

Exhaling, Jake knelt beside her, scooped a handful of rich, dark dirt and sifted it through his fingers. Picking up the small potting trowel, he twirled it in his hand. Then he dug it into the dirt where she pointed. "I...uh... walked in on Dad...and Claudia...kissing."

His face warmed even saying it out loud. He still couldn't believe it and couldn't get the image out of his head.

Tori's head jerked up, and then a grin spread across her face. "Seriously? That's awesome."

He shot her a look. "Yes, seriously, and why is that so awesome?"

"Because they've lost people they've loved, people they expected to spend the rest of their lives with, and now they have a second chance. Besides, they've known each other forever, right?"

"Seems like it. My parents grew up together. Childhood friends. High school sweethearts. Mom met Claudia her freshman year in college—they were roommates and became best friends. Dad met her through Mom.

Then when Claudia married Dennis and moved to Shelby Lake to teach second grade, the four of them were inseparable. Claudia's been like a second mom to us for as long as I can remember."

"Good friends falling in love. It's perfect. They know each other's flaws, and they're still willing to risk their hearts." Tori dug another hole in the flower bed, pulled out a flower and planted it, then looked at him a second before dropping her gaze to the dirt. "Is that possible for us, Jake? Becoming friends, I mean."

He appreciated the clarification, thankful she wasn't asking for more. He was a long way from walking down the aisle. With anyone.

"Let's see how things go." He scrubbed his dirty hands on the legs of his filthy jeans and pushed to his feet. He didn't want to be a jerk, but he needed to be honest, even if it meant hurting her. "I gotta admit our divorce messed me up pretty bad."

"I'm sorry, Jake." She rubbed at the dirt on her fingers, then looked up at him with large, sad eyes. "The last thing I wanted to do was hurt you."

"Hurt me? You wrecked me. If you want to be friends, then you've got to level with me. What did I do wrong?"

Tori gathered the discarded flower trays and smashed them together. She looked at him, her eyes full of sadness. "Nothing. You were…perfect."

He flung his hands in the air, then dropped them to his sides. "Then I don't get it, Tor."

Tori jumped to her feet and slapped the trays on the end of the porch. "If there was any other way, I would have taken it, but I did what I had to do to protect you. To protect your family."

"That's the second time you've said that. How about some clarification? Protect me from what?"

Tori's phone chimed. She pulled it out of her back pocket and looked at the screen. She closed her eyes a second, then opened them and gave him an apologetic look. "I'm sorry, Jake. I am. I know you want answers, and I will tell you everything. I promise." She held up her phone. "But Aunt C's on her way to pick us up. I need to get Annabeth cleaned up before her appointment."

"Fine. But one of these days we're going to talk." Jake reached over and tipped her chin, catching her gaze. "With no interruptions. You owe me that much."

"Yes, I know." She traced the edge of the flower bed with the toe of her leather sandal and crossed her arms over her chest.

"Listen, I'm not sure if you'll want to or if AB will feel up to it, but I'm taking Olivia and Landon fishing after milking to give Tucker a chance to catch up on some sleep. You're welcome to join us if you'd like."

"Are you sure?"

He hesitated a moment, then nodded. "Yes."

What was he doing? Was he a glutton for punishment? Or maybe he needed to have his head examined.

From the moment he met Tori at the NCO club all those years ago, something drew him to her. Despite the pain, despite the ache she carved out in his chest, he couldn't stay away.

When he found out about Dad and Claudia, his first thought had been to talk to Tori. And now, even though he wanted to keep his distance, he couldn't seem to escape the pull she had over him.

And that's what scared him. What if he allowed himself to fall for her again, only to end up with a heart that would be broken beyond repair?

Chapter Seven

What did this city girl know about fishing?

Practically nothing.

Other than going once or twice with Jake while they'd dated, her knowledge of the sport could fill a thimble.

After their conversation, she was a little apprehensive about going, but Annabeth seemed excited, so she'd do her best not to look foolish in front of Jake.

The five-year-old twins and Annabeth ran ahead of Jake and Tori down the rutted tractor path between the cornfields and pasture to Arrowhead Creek, which sliced through the Holland property.

Turquoise-blue skies and warm sunshine offered a perfect day to fish on the bank. Tori adjusted her tote bag filled with sunblock, a blanket, water bottles and snacks.

"Want me to take that?" Jake held out his hand.

"Thanks, but I've got it. You have enough to carry."

He wore a gray T-shirt and navy khakis. Polarized sunglasses and his Ohio State baseball hat shaded his face. A canvas satchel-like tackle bag hung across his chest as he carried five fishing poles in his left hand.

"You're positive you don't mind us tagging along?"

"For the last time, no." A muscle jumped in the side of Jake's jaw, betraying his words.

Yeah, that did little to settle her nerves.

"The fish are going to laugh when they see me casting."

"Relax. I'll help you. Besides, we'll be pretty busy trying to keep those three little monkeys from splashing in the water."

"Maybe we should've gone swimming instead."

"Uh-uh. Nice try, city girl. You're not getting out of it that easily."

They reached the end of the path and needed to cross the barbed wire fence to enter the section of the pasture next to the creek.

"Here, Tori, I'll hold up the fence for you. I have big, strong muscles." Landon curled his arms to show off his biceps, then he lifted the bottom line of fencing.

"Careful of the barbs, buddy." Jake stood behind Landon and helped hold up the wire.

Annabeth and Olivia scuttled underneath as quick as sand crabs, jumped to their feet and shot their arms in the air. "Your turn, Aunt Tori."

Tori eyed the space and glanced at Jake. "How am I supposed to get under there? I'm not exactly built like a five-year-old."

A slow smile creased Jake's face. "And for that, I'm very thankful."

Heat settled across her cheeks. Was he flirting with her?

The man gave her mixed signals.

She stooped down as low as she could and maneuvered under the fence without catching her hair in the wire. She jumped to her feet as Olivia had done, but with much less grace, no doubt.

Once Landon was under, Jake released the bottom wire, set the gear on the other side of the fence, then pushed down on the top line and stepped over like it was no big deal.

The joys of being long-legged.

The kids ran across the pasture and stopped at the creek bank.

A downed oak lay over the water, its branches causing a logjam of sticks and surface foam. A couple of ducks quacked as they floated downstream with their flock of growing ducklings. A frog hopped from one of the logs into the water, creating ripples in the deep pool.

Landon pointed at the water, excitement ringing in his voice. "Uncle Jake, did you see that frog? It was huge!"

"Yeah, I did, buddy." He went down on one knee in front of Landon and placed his hands on his shoulders. "You need to stay away from the water near that tree. It's very deep. Do you understand me?"

The child nodded, but his eyes stayed fixed on the area where the frog had disappeared.

"We'll fish over there." Jake pointed to a safer, shallow area away from the fallen tree.

They walked away from the downed tree. Jake flipped open the flap of his tackle bag and pulled out a small container of worms, helping Landon to slide one on his hook.

Jake scanned the shoreline, then dragged a dry log a safe distance from the water. He helped his nephew to cast his short pole, then instructed him to sit on the log away from the water. While he helped Olivia bait and cast her pole, Tori spread out the blanket on the sun-warmed grass and sat with her knees to her chest as she watched them.

Annabeth wandered over, clutching a fistful of buttercups. "Aunt Tori, I picked you some flowers."

Tori took them and brought them to her nose. "Thanks, sweetie. They're so pretty."

She sat next to Tori on the blanket and rested her head against Tori's shoulder. "I miss my mommy."

"I know, precious. I do, too. But we can talk to her on the computer tonight, remember?" Tori wrapped her arm around the little girl's shoulders and pulled her close. She pressed her lips against Annabeth's blond hair. Snuggling with her niece filled her with bittersweet sadness.

She loved watching Jake with his niece and nephew, but part of her continued to mourn what she'd lost. Seeing Jake's gentleness and patience with the kids showed what a great father he would've been. Was there hope of having a family with him?

"What's the matter, Aunt Tori? You look sad." Annabeth tipped up her head and stared at her.

Tori wrapped her in a hug and tickled her. "How can I be sad when I'm hanging out with the most wonderful girl on the planet?"

She giggled, the sweet sound a balm to Tori's soul. "You're silly."

A quiet click caused Tori's head to turn in Jake's direction in time to see him stowing his phone in his back pocket. Had he taken her picture?

Why?

"Hey, city girl. Ready to show the fish what you've got?"

Tori nodded and laughed. "Won't be much of a show. I hope your expectations are pretty low."

Holding Annabeth's hand, Tori walked down the bank to the water's edge. Jake tossed her a smile that sent her heart tap dancing.

"AB, ready to catch some fish?"

She nodded and put her hand in Jake's large outstretched one. He helped her cast, positioned her on the log next to Olivia and Landon, then turned to Tori. "Your turn."

Tori eyed the water and shook her head. "You guys go ahead. I'll just watch."

Jake rolled his eyes. "Nonsense. This is a full-participation family activity."

Family.

Of course Jake didn't mean that literally. Right? But she'd soak up the moment, squirreling it away in the chest of memories tucked in the back of her heart.

Jake baited Tori's hook, then moved next to her. "Remember how to cast?"

"Is it anything like riding a bike?"

He grinned. "Of course. Except no chance of falling off."

With a shrug, she reached for the pole. Instead of handing it over, Jake held on to it and moved behind her, so close she could smell the scent of his soap and feel his chest pressed against her back. With his muscled arms on each side of her, he cupped his hand over hers as he demonstrated. "This is a spinning reel, so you need to make sure the line is closest to the rod. Then place your hand on the rod and hook your index finger around the line. Be sure you have at least twelve inches of line hanging from the tip of your pole. Open your bail—that curved wire on top—and then bring your rod back over your shoulder. Cast it forward, taking your index finger off the line."

Tori tried to pay attention to Jake's instructions, but his closeness, and the heat of his hand against hers, distracted her from what he was saying.

Why did he have to smell so good?

He released her and stepped back. "Think you can try it now?"

No.

She nodded, hoping she retained some of his words. She focused on the water, mentally recapping what he'd demonstrated, brought her rod over her shoulder, then cast it forward. Her line landed in the middle of the creek with a subtle plink.

"Great job. You're a natural." Jake smiled and gave her shoulder a gentle squeeze.

Another time, she would've turned her face up to his for a kiss, but things were different between them now. She needed to remember that.

A splash sounded off to their left.

"Uncle Jake!" Landon's scream shattered the tranquil stillness, jerking Tori from her thoughts.

Her eyes scoured the bank to see Landon's pole on the ground, but he wasn't anywhere near it. She dropped her rod and ran across the shoreline. "Landon!"

Jake sloshed through the water toward the fallen tree just as Landon's head popped up in the deep pool between the branches.

Jake dived under the water, surfaced a moment later and shouted, "Landon!"

"Over here." A small hand went up on the other side of the heavy oak where he was wedged in the crook of the tree. His arms clung to one of the thicker branches protruding from the trunk.

"Stay there! I'm coming." Jake disappeared again.

Tori scooped up the girls and carried them to the grassy bank away from the water. "Stay here, girls. I'm going to help Jake. Promise not to move?"

The girls nodded, their eyes wide.

Tori hurried back to the water's edge as Jake resurfaced next to Landon and wrapped the kid in his arms. "I've got you, buddy. Let go of the tree."

Landon shook his head, crying. "I can't. My foot's stuck."

Jake disappeared again, then popped back up a few seconds later. Landon released the branch and curled his arms around Jake's neck.

Chest heaving and water streaming off him, Jake carried the child out of the water and set him on the bank. "Are you hurt?"

Landon's bottom lip trembled as he looked down at his bare foot. "I lost my shoe."

"Don't worry about your shoe. We can buy you new ones. Are you okay? Does anything hurt?" Jake knelt in front of him, lifting his arms and legs to check for injuries.

"My elbow." He lifted his arm to show a two-inch bloody scrape. "It hurts."

"Are you sure that's all?" With shaking hands, Jake examined the cut and then scanned the rest of the boy's arms and legs.

Tori grabbed her bag off the blanket and handed a water bottle to Jake. He twisted off the lid and poured water over Landon's cut elbow. Tori handed him a couple of napkins that he pressed against the wound.

She knelt in front of Landon and slipped off his other shoe. "You're going to have to walk barefoot, okay, honey?"

Landon looked down at his bare feet and nodded. He shivered despite the warm sunshine and his teeth chattered. Tori tugged a beach towel out of her bag and wrapped it around his small frame. She sat on the warm grass, crossed her legs, then pulled him into her lap and rubbed his arms to generate some heat.

Jake tipped up his nephew's chin. "What happened, little man?"

"I saw another frog and climbed onto the log to catch it. My foot slipped. I fell into the water."

"Didn't I tell you to stay away from the tree? You could've gotten seriously hurt."

"I'm sorry, Uncle Jake." A tear rolled down the boy's round cheek.

"I know, kiddo. Let's grab our gear and head back to the house." Jake gathered the abandoned poles and reeled in the lines. He dried his face with the hem of his shirt and looked at Tori. "I should've been paying more attention to the kids and…I shouldn't have been so distracted."

She was beginning to hate that word. She shot him a glare. "Are you blaming me for what happened?"

He lifted Landon off her lap and hoisted him on his shoulders. "No, but—"

Not wanting to fight in front of the kids, Tori kept her face neutral and her voice steady, but she glared at Jake. "Let's stick to just working on the fund-raiser. Better yet, I'll text or email you if I have any questions. That way I won't be a *distraction*."

Gritting her teeth against the rest of the words choking her throat, Tori wadded the blanket and jammed it in her bag. She reached for their fishing poles and kept an eye on the girls as they ran down the rutted path to the house.

"Tori…that's not what I meant."

"It's what you said." She quickened her pace to catch up with the girls.

Why was it always two steps forward and about a hundred steps back with him?

Just when she thought they were finding their way back to some semblance of friendship, something tripped them up.

Part of her wondered why she even bothered, but that part managed to get drowned out by her heart that yearned for more.

But what if Jake wasn't able to give her more? Was she setting herself up for more heartbreak?

She'd been praying for this reconciliation for so long, but what if all of these stumbling blocks were God's way of saying no?

Then what?

She didn't know.

After yesterday's fishing fiasco, Jake was surprised when Tori and Annabeth showed up at the house with Claudia for dinner. Her lack of communication with him all day and her cool greeting upon arrival showed she was still upset at his words.

Of course, he was an idiot. Why did his words always seem to stray from what he actually meant?

Why did she have to be so supersensitive to every little thing he said?

That annoyed him.

Could they manage one decent conversation without either of them walking away mad?

He had to admit, though, he wasn't annoyed with her being there.

If he were honest with himself, it was quite the opposite.

He continued to man the grill, but his vantage point also allowed him to watch Tori playing with the kids.

She blew bubbles as they tried popping them. She'd been sure to ask about Landon's elbow, pressing a kiss on his Paw Patrol Band-Aid.

She'd make a great mom someday. But he didn't even want to consider the possibility of her being with anyone but him.

Then he'd need to stop putting his foot in his mouth and step up his game.

His thoughts drifted to their conversation from the other day when she asked if they could be friends.

Sure, he could. But for how long? And at what cost?

Problem was, friends didn't look for excuses to call or text. Friends didn't think about kissing.

He wanted more than friendship. He wanted the past six years back, but that was impossible.

They were different people now. And until she told him why she left in the first place, then they couldn't have a future together.

"Dude, the meat's burning. Focus less on the girl and more on the burgers." The screen door slammed behind Tucker as he stepped out onto the porch pulling a clean T-shirt over his damp hair.

Jake scowled at his brother. "I've got everything under control."

"Famous last words. Just remember I like my burgers

medium well, not charcoaled." Tucker jogged down the deck steps and headed for the yard, pausing to mention something to Tori. She looked at Jake and nodded, her smile disappearing. She handed him the bright blue bottle of bubbles and headed for the deck.

Jake threw up his hands in a "what gives?" motion, but Tucker grinned and snapped a mock salute. Jake scanned the grilling area and looked for something to throw at his brother. Given his recent track record, though, he'd hit one of the kids, and that was the last thing he wanted to happen.

But now he was going to make sure he burned his brother's burger.

Tori joined him at the grill, her face deadpan. "Tucker suggested you might need a hand."

Jake flipped the burgers. Flames lapped at the sizzling meat. "Tucker needs to mind his own business."

"Fine, I'll see if Chuck and Claudia need help in the kitchen." She moved behind him and reached for the door.

Jake grabbed her wrist. "No. Stay. I didn't mean it like that. Tuck, well, he's just being a jerk."

"You sure? I don't want to *distract* you." She shot him a direct look.

He hated hearing his own words being thrown back at him, especially knowing they'd hurt her, but the more he hung around with Tori, the more he was beginning to enjoy the distraction.

So why did he have to be a jerk about it?

"Stay. I mean it." Jake pulled her close and whispered, "Notice how Dad and Claudia are going out of their way not to be near each other? Do they think they're fooling anyone?"

Tori peered around his shoulder through the screen door into the kitchen and smiled. "If you hadn't said anything, I wouldn't be any the wiser. Does Tucker know?"

"I haven't said anything."

"Why not?"

"Not my place."

"You told me."

"Yeah. I was still in shock, I guess. But I'm not in the habit of spreading gossip. They have their reasons for not saying anything and I need to respect that." Jake flipped the burgers one last time and managed to slide them onto the platter without dropping any on the ground, much to the dismay of Poppy and Spencer, Dad's yellow Lab, who positioned themselves at Jake's feet. After several weeks of using only his left hand, he wasn't feeling as clumsy and ridiculous.

Once the eight of them were seated at the picnic table and shooed away the two begging dogs, Dad prayed over the food, then they dug into burgers, baked beans, Dad's special potato salad and watermelon. Annabeth sat between Tori and him with Tucker on his other side while Dad and Claudia corralled Liv and Landon between them.

Chuck snuck a bite of meat under the table to one of the dogs. "So how's the fund-raiser coming along, Tori?"

"Good. We're selling a lot of tickets. Jake's lined up local sponsors and businesses to donate for the auction. We're getting fliers printed up for businesses to post in their windows. We're meeting with another caterer about the menu. We have a meeting with a reporter to share about the program and the purpose of the fund-raiser. Decorations have been ordered. So we're making progress, but there's still quite a bit to be done."

"Let me know what I can do to help."

"Thanks, Chuck. Seems like you have your hands full enough."

A cell phone chimed and Tori pulled hers out of her back pocket, read the display, then looked at them sheepishly. "Sorry, but I have to take this."

Jake pointed his fork at her. "Do so at your own peril. Whoever breaks Dad's 'no phones at the table' rule gets stuck with cleanup."

"I'll risk it. Besides, you definitely want me to take this call." Tori moved away from the table to stand under one of the apple trees with her back to them. Even though he couldn't hear her words, he sensed she wasn't getting good news. She nodded, then her shoulders drooped. She stowed her phone, then caught his gaze and shook her head.

No?

About what?

He moved away from the table and walked over to her. "What's going on?"

"That was my friend, Val—the photographer. The one who'd taken the picture of Micah. Her husband, Josh, is a private investigator. I've asked him to look into this, but he's come up with nothing. No one's seen him since that day. I'm sorry."

Jake wrapped an arm around her shoulders and dropped a kiss on the top of her sun-warmed head. The tea he just downed burned in his stomach. "Not your fault. Thanks for trying. Apparently Micah doesn't want to be found."

"Why not?"

"I don't know."

But deep down he did…and the guilt ate at him.

They returned to the table to find the adults watching. Dad pushed his plate forward and folded his arms on the table. "Everything okay?"

Instead of returning to his dinner, Jake shoved a hand in his front pocket and searched for the right words to say. Tori stood next to him and gave his shoulder a little squeeze.

Claudia climbed away from the table and lowered her voice to a loud whisper. "Hey, kids. Want to go in the kitchen and help me find some ice cream?"

"Yeah!" they cried in unison and scrambled away from the table.

Claudia rested a hand on Dad's shoulder, then as if realizing what she'd done, she jerked it away as her cheeks reddened. She gathered the kids' plates and followed them across the deck and into the house.

Once the door slammed behind them, Jake faced Dad and Tucker. "There's something you need to know. The day after my surgery, Tori showed me some pictures of vets a friend of hers had taken. Tori had told her about the Fatigues to Farming project, and her friend shared her photos." He scrubbed a hand over his face and blew out a breath as he leaned over and braced the end of the table. "And Micah was in one of the photos."

"How do you know it was him?" Tucker pushed his plate aside.

"Because of this." Jake turned his arm over, showing his tat. "He had the same ink."

Dad cleared his throat. A muscle jumped in the side of his jaw. "Why didn't you say something sooner?"

The controlled tone in Dad's voice weighed on Jake's shoulders. Very seldom did Dad use it, but when he did, it was because he was angry and trying not to show it.

"Because I didn't want to get anyone's hopes up. The photos were a couple of months old. Tori's friend's husband is a private investigator. She asked him to look into Micah, but he's come up with nothing."

"You should've told me the minute you saw the photos, Jacob." Dad pounded a closed fist on the table, causing Tori to jump and shoot Jake a startled look. "He's my son."

The frayed edges of pain lacing Dad's voice speared Jake's chest.

Jake schooled his voice and tamped down his own anger and frustration. He forced his words through clenched teeth. "And he's my brother. My fault he's gone. If I hadn't punched him, then maybe he'd still be here…still want to be a part of this family. So it's my responsibility to bring him home. I was trying to protect you from unnecessary hurt."

Dad rested his elbows on the table and dragged his hands over his head. Weariness sagged his shoulders, causing him to look older than his sixty years. "You carry the burdens of this family unnecessarily. Micah's a grown man who made his own choices. And I don't need to be protected. I've dealt with a lot of hurt in my life, and I'm still surviving. We are strong—Holland strong." Dad looked at Tori and held out his hand. "I want to see it. The picture of my son."

Tori pulled out her phone, scrolled through the photos, then handed it to Dad.

Dad cradled the phone, bringing it closer to his face

as if memorizing every pixel in the photo. After a moment, he covered his eyes with a weathered hand and slid the phone back to Tori. "Send that picture to me, please."

"Yes, sir." Tori tapped on her screen.

A few seconds later, Dad's phone chimed.

"Dad, listen—"

Dad held up a hand, then looked at Jake with a stern expression he hadn't seen in years. The rigid jaw and hard eyes—the same look he received upon knowing he'd disappointed his father. "No, *you* listen. Micah is my son and you should've told me."

"I'm sorry, Dad. You're right." Jake's face flamed as he ground his teeth and forced even breaths to settle the raging in his chest. He shot a glance at Tori, who looked at him with a sad smile. He didn't want her pity. And he didn't need to be talked to like he was fifteen again and broke curfew.

"Apology accepted. For months I've prayed, asking God to watch over my boy. Now I know he's been answering my prayers. Micah's alive."

"He was sleeping on a park bench. So apparently he doesn't have the funds to go too far." Jake reached for the iced tea pitcher and refilled his glass, needing something to do with his hands.

"God's watching over him. Now let's work together— as a family this time—and bring him home."

"How? If a private investigator couldn't find him, what makes you think we can?"

"Because I believe God redeems broken families." He thumped his chest. "And I know right here God is going to bring my boy home."

"Micah's in the wind. It's like no one's ever seen him. Not even Evan."

"We know he's alive. Where's your hope, son?"

Hope.

What was wrong with him?

Why couldn't he step out in faith the way Dad and Tucker did? How could they be so certain of something that seemed so impossible?

Chapter Eight

Jake flexed his hand, the skin still pulling around the pink puckered seam across the middle of his palm. An indescribable freedom flowed through him. For the last six weeks, he'd been limited by a splint. And now he could limit it to nighttime use and get back to doing his regular routine.

Well, sort of.

He needed to continue his exercises and be careful not to reinjure his hand.

After listening to the doctor's final instructions, Jake walked out of the office and stepped into the sunshine. He slipped his sunglasses on his face and headed for his truck, only to find Tucker leaning against it holding two Cuppa Josie's to-go cups.

He held up his hand. "Hey, man. Clean bill of health."

Tucker handed him a cup. "Good. Now you can quit slacking and pull your weight around the farm."

"Yeah, like I enjoyed doing nothing." He sipped the coffee.

"I don't know if I'd be complaining about hanging out with a pretty girl all day."

"It's not like that. Tori and I… I mean…yeah, it's not like that."

"Relax, man. I'm just messing with you."

"What are you doing in town? Where are the twins?"

"I dropped Dad off at therapy, went to get a haircut, then swung by the feed store for a new pair of boots— Gwen says hi by the way. The twins are with their aunt Willow. It's her day off, so she called and asked if she could take them for the afternoon. They're making home-made ice cream and slime, hopefully not at the same time."

"Twist your arm, right? Speaking of pretty girls, how is your sister-in-law doing?"

"She's fine." Tucker pushed away from the truck. "Listen, you want to grab a bite or something?"

"Sure. Taking advantage of your freedom?"

"I love the kids—don't get me wrong—but it would be nice to eat a hot meal for a change. How about a pulled pork sandwich from Lena's? I'll buy."

"Sure." Jake clapped his brother on the shoulder. "I give you a lotta credit. Not sure I could handle those two monkeys on my own the way you do."

They stopped at the corner, waited for the light to turn red, then crossed the street, passing by a large foun-tain where a couple of kids splashed in the water.

"You'd find a way if they were your kids. But I'm also fortunate to have you and Dad around to help pick up the slack."

"And don't you forget it."

"Believe me, brother, how could I with you remind-ing me constantly."

They headed to an empty lot next to the river where a red food truck with May the Pork Be With You painted on the side had parked. A couple of white plastic ta-

bles and chairs sat under a pitched awning. The tangy
scents of barbecued pork and french fries scented the
air. Seagulls swooped to snatch pieces of stale bread
Lena had tossed out her back window. Jake's mouth watered as soon as they stepped to the window to order.

Lena Fisher, co-owner with her husband, Lucas,
leaned on the window ledge. "Hey, boys. How's it going?"

Jake smiled at the petite brunette who had been a
couple of years ahead of him in high school. "Hey, Lena.
What's new?"

She scrunched her face into a glare and wagged a
finger at him. "I'm mad at you, Jacob Holland."

"What did I do?"

"More like what you didn't do."

"Okay, fill me in."

"Gwen at the feed store mentioned you're doing a
fund-raiser and you're looking for a caterer. Yet you
haven't called me. What gives?"

"Gwen talks too much." Jake took a take-out menu
off the small counter and stuffed it in his back pocket.
"I'll be sure to give your information to my fund-raiser
coordinator."

"Then I'll be expecting a call."

"Sounds good. How about a couple of pulled pork
sandwiches?"

"Sure thing."

Within minutes, Jake and Tucker were eating their
sandwiches while leaning on the decorative railing on
the river walk by the Shelby River. Midmorning sunshine heated Jake's back. He was half tempted to jump
into the water to cool off.

A couple of kayakers paddled under the bridge to
their right and pulled up along the launch pad.

That gave him an idea.

Jake downed the rest of his sandwich, wadded his wax paper wrapper into a ball and tossed it into the trash can near the food truck. "Hey, man. I need to get going."

"Why? You got a date?"

Heat warmed Jake's face. "Not exactly. Since I'll be back to doing chores tomorrow, I thought I'd see if Tori wanted to go kayaking today."

"Wow. You serious?"

"Yeah."

"Things must be going well with you two."

"She's done a lot with this fund-raiser and she's helping to get us more info on Micah." Jake shrugged as he pulled out his phone and scrolled through his contacts for Tori's number. He tapped on her number and waited for her to answer. When he reached her voice mail, he left a message asking if she'd like to go kayaking, then ended the call and shoved his phone in his back pocket. "I don't know… I've been thinking maybe I should give her a second chance. See what's there, you know?"

"You don't owe me any explanations. Follow your heart."

Jake rolled his eyes. "Really, dude? Now you sound like one of those sappy Lifetime movies Mom used to watch."

"Rayne used to love those, too. I'd sit through them nightly if it meant having her back. I miss her." Tucker stared at the water, twisting his wedding band.

"I know, man. It's tough." Jake turned with his back to the river. He rested his elbows on the railing and looked at his brother. "You know Dad and Claudia have a thing going, right?"

Tucker scoffed and shook his head. "Dad and Claudia? Get out of here. No way, man."

"I'm serious. The morning I did the milking, I accidentally walked in on them kissing."

"What'd they say?"

"Nothing. I don't think they saw me. I bounced pretty quickly."

A grin crossed Tuck's face. "Well, good for them. They deserve it."

"Tori said the same thing."

"You told her?"

"Yeah, I was so caught off guard that I left the farmhouse and took a walk, ending up at Tori's. She was outside planting flowers."

Tucker gave him a knowing look and grinned. "Interesting."

"What about you?"

"What *about* me?"

"Rayne's been gone a couple of years. You think about dating again?"

"No way, man. Not many women want to date a dude who's still hung up on his late wife. Besides, with my crazy hours and the twins…there's no time."

"When the right girl comes along, all of that will fall into place."

"Like Tori did for you. I'm telling you, man. Don't waste what God has given you. If she's the love of your life, then take hold of that and don't let it go."

"Thanks for the sage wisdom, Dr. Tucker." Jake's phone chimed. He pulled it out of his back pocket, looked at the display and grinned. "Looks like I'm going kayaking."

* * *

Tori should've been thrilled. Elated, even. But when Jake called to see if she'd like to go kayaking and maybe talk, she knew it was time. He needed to know the truth. But the thought of his walking away scared her more than anything.

"Are you sure it's not going to tip?" Tori eyed the orange kayak bobbing in the water at the bottom of the launch pad.

"When are you going to trust me?" Jake held out his hand.

With a sigh, she gripped his hand and stepped into the cockpit—wasn't that what he called the sitting area?— one foot at a time, then settled on the cushioned seat. She took the paddle Jake offered and rested it across her lap like he'd directed. She wiped her sweat-slicked hands on the sides of her shorts.

"Check out the footrests so we can see if they need to be adjusted. Those and the side foam knee rests will help with your balancing as you paddle."

She pressed her feet against the rests. "They're fine."

Jake splashed into the water behind her. "I'm going to give you a little shove. You're just going to float a minute. Wait for me before you begin paddling."

Tori's stomach clenched as she drifted farther away from the safety of the boat launch and closer to heavy rocks jutting above the glassy surface.

Battling against lumbering gray clouds, sunlight glazed the cold water, glittering like a razor. Towering pines on each side of the river scraped against the sky. Burdened willows hung over the water's edge, dragging their laden branches against the muddy bank.

Jake drifted closer to her, slid his sunglasses back on his face and grinned. "Ready?"

She nodded, willing her heart rate to slow and wishing some of his enthusiasm would drift her way.

Mimicking him, she gripped the middle of her paddle and dug it into the water on the left side of her kayak, then lifted it in a figure-eight motion and repeated it on the right. Within minutes, she fell into a rhythm and her tense shoulders relaxed. She sat against the cushioned back and breathed in a lungful of fresh air.

A hawk swooped and soared above the bony branches as a flock of mallard ducks—at least that's what Jake had called them—flapped and paddled close to the bank dotted with purple flowers. Cool water dripped off her paddle onto her arms coated with coconut-scented sunblock. She shivered and glanced at the clouding sky. "Looks like it's going to rain."

"Seriously, Tori. You need to relax and enjoy the float down the river."

Easy for him to say.

She rested the paddle in her lap as they drifted silently under an old weathered metal bridge covered in graffiti. Doves cooed from the steel rafters. Trees heavy with white blossoms fragranced the air.

Should've been the perfect date.

Day.

Not date. This wasn't a date.

How many times had she longed for one-on-one time with Jake? And now that she had it, she couldn't relax.

Because she worried it could be her last.

Jake paddled ahead, giving Tori an appealing view of his strong, muscular arms as he dug his paddle into the water and glided effortlessly like the ducks trailing alongside them. He maneuvered his kayak to face her and used his oar as a pointer. "Listen, we're going to hit a patch of rapids, then we'll take a break on that island up ahead. Do exactly as I say, and you'll be fine. Got it?"

Her eyes widened as she stared over his shoulder at the churning frosted water. Her heart rate picked up speed as she gripped the sides of the kayak. "Don't leave me."

He slid his sunglasses on top of his head and leveled her with a direct look. "I'd never leave you. Someday you'll believe that."

"What if I flip?"

"Do as I say, and you'll be fine. These rapids aren't that bad. I promise."

She wanted to believe him, to lean into his words, but the water rushed over surface rocks and sloshed against the sides of her boat, causing fear to bubble in her throat.

He pointed his paddle toward the quickly approaching rapids. "Stay calm. You may get a little wet, but you'll dry." He winked and shot her a half grin. "Follow me through the middle. Use your paddle only to steer away from obstacles. Remain seated and enjoy the ride."

She bumped and bounced through the rapids as she seized her paddle and kept her eyes on Jake. Her kayak swiveled sideways, the front knocking against a protruding rock. "Jake!"

Jake whipped around at the panic in her voice. "Tori, relax. You're almost out of them. Push the blade of your paddle toward the bow…the front. That'll turn you away from the rock."

She followed his directions. Within seconds she shot through the rapids into calmer water. She released her paddle, setting it beside her, and buried her face in her shaking hands. Her chest heaved as she forced her breathing to slow, to return to normal.

"Tori, look out!"

She jerked her head up as a log floated toward her. Startled, she reached for her paddle but ended up knocking it in the water instead. "Oh, no!"

She leaned over the side of the kayak to grab it, and as her fingertip grazed the foam grip, the kayak tipped. Before she could right herself, the kayak flipped over, launching her in the water. Her arms flailed as she went under. She pushed herself to the surface and choked as river water jammed her throat and lodged in her right ear. As she treaded water, her head knocked against the side of the capsized death trap.

"Tori!" Jake slipped over the side of his kayak and swam toward her. He gripped her under her arms and hauled her to his chest. "Are you okay?"

Rubbing her forehead, she coughed and nodded. "Yes, except for my ego."

"Bruised egos will heal. Let me look at your forehead." He pried her fingers away and touched a tender area. She winced. "You have a red mark, but the skin's not broken."

He released her and flipped her kayak right-side up. He retrieved the wayward paddle and dropped it inside. "Want to learn how to enter a kayak from the water?"

"Is that my only option?"

"How are your swimming skills?"

"Much better than kayaking."

"Well, the island's over there. This water's not very deep. If you want to swim over, I'll grab these and bring them to shore."

"I'll pull my own." Reaching for the carrying handle on the bow, Tori swam until her feet could touch the rocky bottom. She splashed through the water, slipping on the slick rocks, and dragged her kayak onto the pebbled shore. She unzipped her life jacket, toed off her wet outdoor sandals and collapsed on the grassy bank. The sunshine heated her chilled body. Northwestern Pennsylvania river water wasn't very warm in June. Muscles she hadn't used in a while quivered from exhaustion.

Jake hauled his kayak next to hers, dug a couple of waterproof bags out of one of the compartments and tossed them next to her. He dropped beside her, pulled a red plaid blanket out of one, shook it out on the grass and invited her to sit. Reaching for the other bag, he took out two bottles of iced tea, a couple of sandwiches, a container of strawberries and a bag of what looked like smashed brownies.

"What's all of this?"

"Food." He shot her a smirk. "Figured you might've worked up an appetite."

"Don't you have to do something to work up an appetite? All I did was flip my kayak."

"And you handled it like a champ. You didn't panic and made it—and your kayak—safely to shore." He handed her a bottle of tea.

She smiled her thanks and allowed his compliment to warm her. She uncapped the bottle and read the words inside the cap.

Everything you've always wanted is within distance.

If only.

Jake plopped on the blanket next to her, drew up his knees, then—using his opened bottle—he pointed to the arch of two broad oak trees on each side of the water.

"See those two oaks? And how it looks like they're growing toward each other?"

Tori nodded.

"It's called Bridal Bend. When my grandparents were teenagers, they weren't allowed to date because my grandma's wealthy family felt my grandpa, a lowly farmer's son, wasn't good enough for their daughter. This creek separated both of their properties, so they used to sneak off to these oak trees to hang out. My great-grandfather found out and forbid her to see my grandfather. As soon as my grandma graduated high school, she was going to be sent to stay with family in upstate New York for the summer. So the night of her graduation, they came to this spot with one of my distant cousins who was a young pastor and eloped on this island." Jake stood and held out a hand. "Come with me. I want to show you something."

Tori capped her bottle and set it on the blanket, then took Jake's hand as he led her to the broad oak.

Without letting go of hers, he trailed his other hand over the bark until he came to a bare patch. "Here. Check this out."

She took a step closer to the tree and traced a jaggedly carved heart in the bark. "JH + VL 1954."

"Jacob Holland—I'm named after my grandfather— and Virginia Larson. Everyone called her Ginny. They were married fifty years until my grandma died of a heart attack fourteen years ago. Granddad couldn't bear to live without her and ended up passing away a month later. They started the Holland Family Farm with only a couple of cows and a handful of chickens and later passed it on to my dad."

"That's a beautiful story." She traced the initials again. Initials that could be hers and Jake's.

"I've always admired them. They overcame obstacles to be together. And from the stories they've shared, their lives weren't always easy, but they were there for each other. No matter what. They believed in the promises they made to each other in 1954 and did what it took to keep those vows. Our last family celebration with them was their fiftieth wedding anniversary."

"Sounds like they left behind a great legacy."

"They were like the American dream—they loved God, their family and the farm." Jake turned and took Tori in his arms. He lifted his hands and cupped her jaw, caressing her cheeks with his thumbs. "I want that, Tori. With you. I always have."

Before she could respond, he slid his fingers away from her face and threaded them through the tangles of her wet hair. His head lowered, and he covered her mouth with his.

She cupped his face and allowed his cool lips to kiss her. For a moment, she savored the security of his embrace, the strength of his arms. For a moment, she breathed in the scents of sunshine and fresh air she associated with him. For a moment, she allowed herself to give in to those dreams of wondering what it would be like to have him hold her again.

She gentled the kiss, then pulled away, pressing her forehead against his chest, her hand over his heart and feeling the rushing beats against her palm. His ragged breathing reminded her he wasn't as immune to her presence as he wanted her to believe.

Her heart pounding in her ears, she looked at him, his eyes dark and stormy.

She had to tell him.

"Oh, Jake." She stroked her fingers through his wet hair. "I want that, too. I do..."

His jaw tightened as his hold around her loosened. "Why am I sensing a *but* coming?"

Tori lowered her eyes. "It's just...there's something... I need to tell you something. Something I should've told you a long time ago."

Jake lowered his hands and took a step back, pressing his back against the sturdy oak. "This doesn't sound good."

She hated the gap between them. The gap that always seemed to be there. And now her words were going to cause a divide that may be too wide to bridge back together.

Tears blurred her vision. A gust blew off the water, plastering her wet clothes to her like a second skin. Clouds forced away the sun, dropping them in the shadows.

"Just tell me already. The silence is driving me crazy."

She blew out a breath and caught his gaze. "About three weeks after you'd been deployed, I'd woken up in the middle of the night bleeding and in a lot of pain. I had to be taken to the hospital."

"What happened?" He frowned, but the tenderness in his voice nearly unraveled the frayed knot tethering her emotions.

"I had a miscarriage. I—I lost our baby." A tear trailed down her cheek.

Jake's eyes widened. "Our what?" He dragged a hand through his wet hair. "Our baby? You were pregnant and didn't tell me?"

She shook her head. "I didn't even know I was pregnant. It was early. Too soon."

"But since then? Why wasn't I ever informed? You could've sent a message. Tori, I should've known. I would've moved mountains to be there. Are you okay? Now, I mean?"

"I'm fine. Physically. But there's more. Somehow my dad found out—Kendra promises she never called him—and he came to see me at our apartment. I was vulnerable and lonely. And so sad. I missed you so much—I hated being apart from you. And my heart ached. Dad tried to talk me into coming back home, and when that didn't work, he threatened to go after you and your family."

"Go after me? That's ridiculous. You're joking, right?"

She shook her head. "I'm serious."

"Why? What kind of person does that? Sounds like something out of a bad movie."

"My father was very controlling, and he didn't like it that neither of his daughters were under his thumb."

"You should have told me. I would have worked out a way to get home and help you."

"My dad—"

"Let me guess—he told you not to contact me? He'd make things difficult for me, too?"

She nodded. "I knew you wanted to make the Marine Corps your career, and I didn't want to be the one to ruin that for you."

Jake released a harsh laugh. "This is ridiculous, Tori. Your father may have been wealthy, but he does not have that much influence with Uncle Sam. He was all talk and you fell for it. You threw away our marriage. You broke your promise. To me. To us."

"I did it to protect you, Jake." Her voice choked as tears streamed down her face.

"I didn't need protecting, Victoria. I was a United States marine. I would've handled it. But you didn't even let me try."

"I was only twenty-two, afraid and lonely. And stupid."

"No argument here. You wanted your dad's love so badly that you threw away what I offered freely without condition. I love… I loved you, Tori. I meant those words I said when I promised to love and honor you. And if I had to protect you from your own family, I would have done so, but you didn't even give me a chance to prove it. You just…walked away."

"I'm sorry, Jake." A sob shuddered in her chest. Turning her back to him, she balled her hand and pressed it against her mouth.

Telling him the truth was supposed to relieve her of the weight of her guilt that had been pressing on her heart.

But instead it'd pushed him further away. He'd only see her for the silly, immature girl she once was.

Tears coursed down her cheeks faster than she could wipe them away. She swallowed several times, trying to regain control of her emotions, but the look of raw pain on his face stamped in her memory caused her to grieve all over again.

She cried for their lost dreams, their desire to have a family someday and the innocence of their crazy, almost reckless courtship.

Jake touched her shoulder and turned her, wrapping

his arms around her. She buried her face into his chest and allowed him to swaddle her in the cradle of his embrace. She tightened her arms around his waist and clung to him as the tears flowed unchecked.

He sniffed quickly and she turned her face to see him wiping his own tears with the pad of his thumb.

He wanted what his grandparents and his parents had.

With her.

But now that wish would fly away in the wind like dandelion dust. Her confession ruined that. And she had no one to blame but herself.

What should have been a perfect day ended in disaster. And there were some problems she just couldn't paddle back from.

Chapter Nine

Somehow Jake had to get past the hurt and adjust to the fact that his ex-wife was going to be his neighbor and nothing more.

The promises they'd made to each other in that tiny chapel had been broken. Because of fear. Because she believed her father's word over his. And she'd never given Jake a chance to prove he could take care of her.

At least now he knew why she'd left.

Question was, could he do what it would take to keep her from walking away again?

Did he even want to try?

Could he trust her to stay, to be there to share all of his heart?

He wasn't sure.

She didn't believe his words—his promises—and he couldn't trust her to stay.

And the pain she'd gone through with losing her—no, their—baby, well, he struggled to wrap his head around that.

He'd almost been a father.

One more life God had taken from him.

Jake closed his laptop and shoved it onto the coffee table. He leaned forward, resting his elbows on his knees, and rubbed his eyes.

He hadn't been able to focus on the fund-raiser notes for the past hour so why bother pretending? They had a bunch of things left to do, but honestly he was so ready to be done with the whole thing.

To get back to life before Tori returned.

But what would that look like?

Spencer's ears perked as headlights spanned across the front of the house and tires crunched the gravel in the driveway.

"Sounds like Dad's home, ole boy." Jake scratched the Lab's head.

Spencer shot off the couch as the door between the garage and the laundry room opened.

Dad appeared in the doorway wearing tan dress pants and a light blue dress shirt opened at the throat—clothes he typically wore to church.

"Nice threads. What's the occasion?"

Dad scowled and looked at his watch. "What are you doing up? It's past midnight."

"Couldn't sleep." Jake rubbed his forehead. A dull ache pounded behind his skull.

"What's on your mind?"

"What makes you think there's something on my mind?"

"Well, for starters, you answered my question with a question. Plus, you've been moody and distracted all week. Something going on between you and Tori?"

"No."

Absolutely nothing.

Dad wandered over to the couch and sat next to him.

Spencer jumped up between them and rested his chin on Dad's knee. Dad leaned his head against the back of the couch and looked at Jake. "Kid yourself all you want, but you can't fool your old man."

Jake released a sigh. "Last week when Tori and I went kayaking, we ended up at Bridal Bend. I told her I wanted what Granddad and Grandma had...with her."

"Judging by your hound dog expression, that didn't go over well."

"She confessed why she'd left." Jake pushed to his feet and moved in front of the window, staring out into the darkness punctuated by the barn lights. "When we were married, after I'd been sent overseas, Tori ended up in the hospital."

"What happened?"

Jake's throat thickened as tears pressed against the backs of his eyes. "She lost—" His voice cracked. Horrified at losing it in front of his father, Jake scrubbed a hand over his face and exhaled a deep sigh. "She lost our baby."

Even now, the words still seemed so surreal.

Dad moved behind him and rested a hand on his shoulder, their reflections mirrored in the windowpane. "Son, I'm sorry. So sorry. And you just found out?"

Jake nodded, rubbing his eyes with a thumb and forefinger. He dragged a hand through his tangled hair. "After she was released from the hospital, her dad paid her a visit—Tori still doesn't know how he found out. Basically the jerk blackmailed her into ending our marriage."

"How so?"

Jake's voice rose as he paced while relaying what Tori had told him a week ago.

"Sounds like she was scared and didn't know what to do." Dad shoved his hands in his trouser pockets and jingled his change.

"But that's the thing, Dad, she never gave me a chance to show her. She sent those papers without even talking to me. I could've taken emergency leave and been there for her, fought for her."

"Why didn't you do it anyway?"

"My commanding officer said she'd file harassment charges if I tried."

"Sounds like her father's words. Not hers."

Footsteps sounded on the stairs, and then Tucker appeared in the family room rubbing his eyes and wearing a wrinkled yellow T-shirt with a green John Deere logo and tan cargo shorts, his hair resembling a cactus. "What's with the yelling?"

Jake dropped on Dad's favorite recliner. "Sorry, man. Didn't mean to wake you. Dad asked about Tori and I guess I got a little heated."

"Don't worry about me, but if you wake the twins, they're all yours until you get them back to sleep." He sat on the edge of the coffee table and batted at his brother's knee. "What's going on?"

Suddenly drained, Jake gave him the condensed version.

Tucker let out a low whistle and shook his head. "That's tough. Sorry, man. What's your next step?"

Jake shot him a look. "Next step for what?"

"Getting Tori back, of course."

"What makes you think I want her back? Did you hear what I told you?"

"Dude, you've been moping since that kayak trip. I get how it feels when life punches you in the gut, but now you have a choice to make—allow the past to keep you from having the future you want or get up and fight for it. I'm sorry she hurt you. It stinks. Really, it does, but it's in the past. You can't change it. Learn from it, forgive her and move forward."

"You make it sound so easy."

"And you're complicating it like a fifteen-year-old. Dial down the drama."

"This is more than a high school crush, you jerk. She was my wife." Jake punched his brother in the shoulder.

Tucker slugged him back. "Then man up and fight for her. Talk to her. Listen to her. Show her you want her in your life. Chicks dig that kind of stuff."

"Have plenty of experience with chicks, do you?"

Tucker held up his left hand where his ring remained despite the years since his wife's passing. "Hey, Rayne and I celebrated ten years before I lost her. How many anniversaries have you had?"

"Low blow." Jake tossed a throw pillow at Tucker's head.

He ducked and caught it one-handed, then dropped it on the couch, barely missing Spencer. "If you want it, make it happen. Back me up, Dad." Then, as if noticing Dad's dress clothes for the first time, Tucker whistled. "Yo, Pops, what's up with the Sunday threads on a Thursday night?"

"I went out. You got a problem with that?"

Tucker held up his hands in mock surrender. "Nope, not at all." He belly flopped onto the couch, folded his hands under his chin and fluttered his eyelashes.

"Where'd you go? Who were you with? How'd it go? Tell me all the deets."

Dad laughed and pushed him off the couch. "You're such an idiot at times, you know that?"

"Of course. But this family could use a little more of my idiocy. And more laughter." Tuck sat up and stretched out on the other end of the couch, folded his hands behind his head, and crossed his feet at the ankles on the coffee table. He looked at Jake and smirked. "Hey, Jake, know who has a great laugh?"

"Who, Tuck?"

"Claudia. Claudia Gaines has a great laugh. Wouldn't you agree?"

Jake grinned at the redness tinging Dad's ears. "Why yes, I would. What about you, Dad? Do you think Claudia has a great laugh?"

"Knock it off. Both of you." Dad wagged his finger at the two of them, then snapped off the lamp next to the couch, leaving only the moonlight streaming through the open bay window to light the room. "I'm going to bed. You two clowns can lock up and turn out the rest of the lights."

"I saw you two. Kissing. A couple of weeks ago." Jake's words bounced off Dad's retreating back.

Thrusting his hands in his pockets and with his back to them, Dad laughed quietly and shook his head. He turned to face them. "And here we thought we were being so careful."

"What can I say? I have the skills of a ninja." Jake stood and shrugged.

Dad leaned against the door frame and crossed his arms over his chest. "So instead of saying something to me, you blabbed to your brother."

Grinning, Jake shook his head. "Nah, he was working. So I told Tori. Then I told Tuck."

"Awesome. Why not just post it on Facebook?"

Jake stroked his chin. "I considered it but I couldn't find the right emoji for 'my dad's having a secret fling and won't tell his family about it.'"

"It's not a fling." Dad shot them a direct no-nonsense look.

Jake's smile faded. "Then what is it? Is it serious?"

"Serious enough for this." Dad reached into his pocket, pulled out a box and tossed it to Jake.

He opened the small rose-colored velvet box and stared at the solitaire diamond seated in the ivory-colored cushion. He turned to show it to Tucker.

"Whoa, Dad." Tucker patted the couch. "I think you need to share a few more details."

"What's to tell? She's been one of my closest friends for over thirty years. She was an amazing friend after I lost your mother. Then after Dennis died, we grew closer. Things just kind of happened."

"How long have things 'just kind of happened'?" Jake made air quotes over his father's words.

"About six months."

"Six months?" Jake and Tucker spoke in unison.

Dad chuckled. "Apparently you're not the only stealthy one."

"Sneaky's more like it." Tucker pushed to his feet. "And right under our noses."

"I picked up the ring tonight and planned to talk to you guys before I proposed."

Jake and Tucker looked at each other, then Jake wagged a finger between them. "You don't need our permission."

"Your blessing would be nice."

"You don't need that either. Claudia's cool. She's been like a second mom to us since we were kids. But this is your life."

Dad looped his arms around Jake's and Tucker's shoulders. "Thanks. Losing Lily was the hardest thing I've had to go through, and she will always have a place in my heart, but I can't stop living because she's gone. Claudia and me...well, we're good together. And I love her."

"There you go. That's the only reason you need."

"I know you boys can have your second chances, too."

Tuck held up his hands and took a step back. "Don't look at me. I have my hands full with work, the twins and watching out for my older brother."

Dad raised an eyebrow and gave a little shake of his head. "You never know, Tuck. When the right woman comes along..."

"Yeah, well, let's get you married off and then figure out how to prevent Jake and Tori's stupidity from keeping them apart before we even think about me."

"Let's call it a night." Dad whistled for Spencer, who shot off the couch to follow him up the stairs.

Behind him, Tuck started to sing, "Dad and Claudia sitting in a tree. K-I-S-S-I-N-G..."

"Knock it off. Or you're going to be bunking in the barn."

"Hey, camping in the hayloft like we did when we were kids."

Jake laughed, but Dad's words about not living in the past replayed through his head. If his father could find love again after everything he had lost, then what was holding Jake back?

Keeping a smile in place was going to be Tori's toughest job of the day.

Sitting on one of the blush-colored upholstered armless chairs in the showroom at Emily's Bridal did little to soothe her wounded heart.

She was thrilled for Aunt Claudia. She was. And she'd do whatever it took to make her day with Chuck special.

They deserved it.

But the thought of spending the day talking flowers, trying on dresses and sampling wedding cakes…well, that carved an ache in Tori's chest.

Recessed lighting and glittering chandeliers reflected off the floor-to-ceiling mirrors to capture the beauty of the satin and beading of the wedding gowns positioned on mannequins lining the cream-colored walls.

She hadn't been a typical bride when she and Jake had made the rash decision to elope. No dress fittings, addressing invitations, choosing a menu for the reception. None of it.

She'd worn a simple but lovely white sundress with a light blue bolero sweater borrowed from her sister and earrings that had been her mother's—a gift her father had given her for her sixteenth birthday. Jake had stopped at a flower shop near the base and bought her a small hand-tied bouquet of white rosebuds, baby's breath and blue forget-me-nots, claiming every bride needed flowers.

She'd been so happy that she hadn't cared about not having a "real" wedding.

If only that happiness had lasted.

Since their recent kayaking disaster, her communication with Jake had taken place via email or texting. Even though fund-raiser plans were coming together, she wanted to review some things face-to-face. But that was kind of tough when every time she stopped by the farm he was on the tractor out in the field, at the feed store or simply mysteriously out of sight. With the fund-raiser only a couple of weeks away, she was running out of time.

Thing was, she missed him.

Simple as that.

And there wasn't anything she could do until he was ready to talk in person.

Her eyes strayed to an oversize print of four men in suits hanging above the tuxedo rental section.

Or could she?

What if...

Tori pulled out her phone and made a few notes.

"What do you think?"

Tori looked up at the sound of Aunt Claudia's voice and sucked in a breath. "You look...incredible."

Her aunt stood on the circular platform in front of a trio of mirrors wearing a sleeveless A-line dress with a lacy beaded bodice and layers of chiffon over satin that fell past Claudia's knees in a layered handkerchief hem.

Aunt Claudia looked over her shoulder and admired the back of the dress in the mirror, then she turned to face Tori, her eyes glistening. "When Dennis and I got married, we had a huge wedding. This time, I want something smaller, simpler. But this dress..."

Tori rose to her feet and reached for Claudia's hand. "It's perfect. You can still have a lovely wedding in Chuck's backyard with the apple trees in the background like you want. With your hair up, a pair of dangly diamonds and strappy sandals with rhinestones, you'll take Chuck's breath away."

Aunt Claudia winked. "That's the whole point, isn't it?"

Tori's eyes filled with tears. "I'm so happy for you. Both of you."

"He's a good man." Claudia stepped off the platform and reached for a tissue to dab the tear trailing down Tori's cheek. "Jake's a good man, too. I've loved those boys from the time they were born. Give him time, sweetheart. He'll come around."

"I don't know. I hurt him pretty badly."

"With prayer and time—sometimes a whole lot of both—hurts will heal."

A seed of hope bloomed in Tori's chest. She wanted to hold on to Claudia's words and cling to them, but part of her wondered if she wasn't setting herself up for major disappointment. Especially after Jake's absence the past week.

Tori's phone rang. She picked it up and frowned. She didn't recognize the number. "Hello?"

"Victoria Lerner, my dear girl, what on earth are you doing holing up in the boonies?"

The raspy voice could belong only to Sophie Mays, her former employer, and the closest she had to a mother until being reunited with Aunt Claudia.

"Sophie! So great to hear from you. I didn't recognize your number. How are you?"

"Dreadful, darling, simply dreadful."

Tori smiled at Sophie's flair for drama. She could imagine her friend pacing and throwing her hands in the air. "What's wrong?"

"Kiki and I have parted ways."

"Sorry to hear that."

Aunt Claudia motioned she was returning to the dressing room. Tori nodded, mouthed an apology for the phone call and returned to her chair.

"Oh, don't be. It's all good. Actually, the little minx ran off and got married. Eloped! Can you imagine?"

Actually, she could.

"So, anyway, I'm calling because I want you to come back and work with me. Partners. Fifty-fifty. People are wondering where you disappeared to."

"You know I needed to come to Shelby Lake to take care of family business."

"I know, love, I know. But I'm desperate."

Somehow she couldn't see herself returning to Pittsburgh and calling it home. In the two months she'd been in Shelby Lake, she'd come to love the small-town pace. And now that she'd gotten to know her aunt again, did she really want to leave?

And there was Jake.

If she left, then they wouldn't have a chance. Jake wasn't willing to leave his farm. Especially now with his veterans project getting started.

And she had Annabeth to think about.

"Hello? Did I put you to sleep, darling?"

"No, sorry. I was thinking about your offer."

"More like trying to think of a gentle way to let me down, aren't you? What'd you do—rope yourself a hunky country boy?"

Tori laughed. "A lot of reasons are keeping me here, but Jake… Well, let's just say that's one of the best reasons to get me to leave. If things were different, Sophie, I would jump at the chance to work with you. But I can't leave right now. I'm committed to a project and I must see it through. Besides, my aunt is getting married. In fact, I'm at the bridal salon with her right now."

"Darling, why didn't you say something sooner? Listen, you go be with your aunt, but promise me you'll call later. I won't take no for an answer. And I want to hear more about—"

Tori cut her off before she could ask anything further. "I'll call you later. I promise, Sophie."

"Talk to you soon."

The call ended before Tori could reply. Leave it to Sophie to get in the last word.

Tori stowed her phone in her purse and returned her attention to her aunt, who had changed into her yellow sundress and leather sandals and was paying for her wedding dress.

"Sorry about that. I didn't mean to ignore you, but I needed to take that call."

"No worries. Everything okay?"

"Yes, that was Sophie Mays."

"Your former boss?"

"Yes, she called to offer me a promotion, sort of. She wants me to be her partner in the company."

"Wow, Tori. That's a big deal. Are you going to take it?"

"I told her I had other commitments right now, but she made me promise to call her later."

"So you didn't say no."

"It's difficult to tell Sophie no, but I'll call later and hear her out. But my home is now here."

Claudia wrapped an arm around her. "Good. Call me selfish, but I'm not ready to lose you again."

"Dad was wrong in the way he handled things."

"I should've been more assertive, insisted to see you

girls more often, but your father held a grudge about something that seems so silly now. But that's in the past. We can't change our mistakes. We can only learn from them and work hard not to repeat them." Claudia took the satin garment bag from the bridal consultant and threaded her arm through Tori's. "Let's grab some lunch at Cuppa Josie's before we head to the flower shop."

They left the air-conditioned boutique and stepped out into the blazing sunshine. Tori slid her sunglasses on her face. As she glanced down the sidewalk, her heart jammed between her ribs.

Jake.

And he wasn't alone.

He laughed, then wrapped an arm around the shoulders of a petite brunette outside Cuppa Josie's.

No wonder she hadn't heard from him all week. He'd been occupied with someone else.

Tears flooded her eyes, but she forced her practiced smile in place, thankful for her sunglasses to shield her pain. This was Claudia's day and she wasn't going to be a downer even if it meant spending time later stitching the pieces of her broken heart back together.

Maybe Sophie's timing was perfect.

If Jake was interested in someone else, then perhaps she should consider seeing what Sophie had to offer because living next to him while he saw someone else would be torture.

And how could she recover from that?

Chapter Ten

If Tori wanted to become successful in her career, she was going to have to learn to juggle because she wasn't doing such a stellar job of it these days. Between helping Aunt Claudia with last-minute wedding details and putting the final touches on the fund-raising campaign, she was dropping balls right and left.

But at least now she had her own space to work in. Maybe she'd end up doing a better job of containing everything.

Even if her space was filled with boxes and furniture needing to be arranged.

She had an hour before she needed to meet with the caterer—a friend of Jake's who owned a food truck or something like that. Handing that task off to him had taken one more thing off her plate.

Maybe she had enough time to empty a few boxes and create some sort of living space before Aunt Claudia returned with Annabeth, who was playing at the farm with the twins.

When the moving company called to say they'd be delivering her furniture and belongings a day early, she had to scramble to be at the house on time. And she had no time to round up help with unloading the truck. Thankfully the two men who worked for the moving company took pity on her and carried in the heavy stuff.

But after two hours of carrying boxes, she was beat.

Didn't help that she woke up with a headache and scratchy throat.

How had she survived all winter without getting sick, but managed to catch a summer cold?

She gazed at her bare mattress pinned between the wall and the beige sectional. If only she could throw a blanket over it and curl up for an hour. Just a quick catnap to get rid of the fatigue she hadn't been able to shake since forcing herself out of bed this morning when her phone rang.

But there was no time.

She had a house to put together. A wedding to finish planning. And the fund-raiser to complete.

And less than two weeks to finish everything.

Before she could do anything else, she needed to find her purse for some ibuprofen to dull the throbbing in the back of her head.

And water. With lots of ice.

Her throat felt as if she'd swallowed razor blades.

After finding her purse and downing medicine, she smothered a yawn and rubbed a thumb and forefinger over her burning eyes.

What was her problem today? She needed to get it together. Too many people depended on her.

Another glance at her phone showed she had forty-five minutes until her meeting with the caterer.

What was her name again?

Lizzie? Lorna? Lori?

Her head ached trying to remember.

She pulled up this morning's to-do list—finalize details with caterer, take Annabeth and Olivia to Emily's Bridal for dress fittings, follow up with fund-raiser sponsors about their ad information before sending everything to the printer, and pick up decorations for the wedding and reception.

The list continued, but the more she read, the deeper she sank into the chair that matched her sectional.

How could Sophie consider her for partner if working on two different projects at once reduced her to putty?

Her conversation with Sophie had gone well, especially after she'd told her about the Fatigues to Farming awareness campaign. Even though Sophie did PR for published authors, she wanted to expand her company, which was where Tori would come in. She'd coordinate awareness campaigns for voices that struggled to be heard.

Her dream job.

But it would mean leaving Shelby Lake.

She couldn't think about that right now. Too many other things needed her attention.

If her head would stop throbbing, she could think.

Maybe a ten-minute catnap would help. Just enough to let the medicine clear her brain fog.

She tucked her feet up under her thighs, folded her arms on the chair, rested her head and closed her eyes.

Just ten minutes...

The pounding.

And the ringing.

Make it stop.

Tori's eyes jerked open, then she winced against the sudden brightness.

The dull thud in the back of her head had escalated into a full-blown explosion of pain. She struggled to focus, but her eyes burned. A chill snaked over her skin, sending a shiver down her spine. As she tried to stand, her knees weakened like overcooked pasta.

Where was that ringing coming from?

Her phone.

Where was it?

Through bleary eyes, she searched the chair but couldn't find it. It sounded muffled.

Pounding.

More ringing.

The peal of the doorbell.

She staggered through the maze of boxes until she reached the door. She wrenched it open and sagged against the door frame, throwing an arm over her eyes to shield them from the stabs of light. A shadowy form stood on her front porch.

"Step…away…from…the…doorbell."

"Tori, what's wrong?"

"Jake." Her mouth felt dry. She tried to swallow but winced against the flames licking her throat. She turned away from the door. Where was her water bottle?

Staggering back to the living room, she found it and tried to drink, but her throat felt like it had been stuffed with rocks.

Jake touched her shoulder. "Tori, what's going on? What's all your stuff doing here? Why didn't you ask for help?"

Tori held up a hand. "Shh."

Jake cupped her face. "Have you been drinking?"

She nodded, holding up her water bottle. "Trying to, but my throat...hurts."

Why did her voice sound so hoarse?

Jake took the bottle from her and sniffed it.

What a weird thing to do.

He placed his palm against her forehead. She sighed as the coolness of his touch offered relief against her sweltering skin and reached for his other hand to press against her cheek. "That feels good."

"You're burning up. I'm taking you to the clinic."

"No, I have to meet the caterer—your friend. The pig truck girl. Can't remember her name."

"Tori, honey, that's why I'm here. Lena called because you missed the appointment. She tried calling... I did, too. But you didn't answer, so I came to find you."

"What? No. I have to finalize the order today. She's leaving. Going someplace. I can't remember where. It hurts to think. Then the girls need dresses. And the ads. Plus decorations. But then the movers called to say they were delivering today instead of tomorrow." Tori's voice choked, and tears leaked down her face as she cradled her head. "But this headache wouldn't go away, so I closed my eyes for only a few minutes. Then I could handle everything. Instead, I've ruined it. No wonder you don't want me around."

Tugging her against his chest, Jake finger-combed her tangled hair away from her face. As his arms wrapped around her, drawing her deeper into his embrace, she leaned against him, hoping some of his strength could wear off on her. She needed to pull herself together.

Jake pulled away, sending a chill against her skin, and wiped away her tears with his roughened thumb.

"I've taken care of the caterer, and I'm going to take care of you, too. But first you need to see a doctor. Where's your phone? What about your purse?"

"I dropped my phone. I was looking for it when you came to the door."

Jake found her phone, her purse and her flip-flops. He held on to her while she shuffled her feet into her shoes, then guided her to his truck. Her teeth chattered and goose bumps pebbled her skin despite the sunshine heating the cab. He pulled out a blanket from behind his seat, shook it out and tucked it around her.

As he backed out of her driveway, she leaned her head against the window. From the moment she offered to oversee the fund-raiser, she wanted to prove her worth, to prove she had value, to prove she'd changed. But all she managed to prove was she was a walking disaster who needed to be rescued once again.

Jake was in trouble.

It was the second time he had to rescue Tori, as she called it. Third, if he counted their kayaking misadventure. And each time he felt like his gut had been twisted inside out.

He slouched in the club chair in the corner of the farmhouse guest room meant more for decoration than comfort and watched Tori sleep.

Her damp hair matted around her face—her fever must have broken in the night. The paleness of her skin emphasized the dark shadows around her eyes.

But she still looked beautiful to him.

When she woke up, would she remember the trip to the ER, the stop at the pharmacy for antibiotics for strep throat, then being helped upstairs to recuperate at the farmhouse until she was no longer contagious?

Why hadn't she asked for help instead of trying to do everything on her own?

Maybe because he'd acted like a stubborn jerk by not talking to her since their kayaking trip.

"Where am I?" Tori's groggy voiced jerked him out of his thoughts.

Jake pushed to his feet, an ache arching across his lower back, and moved to her bedside. "You're at the farmhouse. In the guest room." He reached for the insulated cup filled with ice water, and handed it to her. "How are you feeling?"

She struggled to sit up, took the water and sipped it, then handed it back to him before falling back against the pillow. "Tired. And my throat hurts."

"Not surprising, considering you have a nice case of strep."

"Strep? Where did I pick up that?" She frowned, then closed her eyes.

"Hard to say. Could've been anywhere. It's highly contagious. That's why you're here and not at Claudia's. We can't have the bride sick before her wedding day."

Tori's eyes jerked open and her hand flew to her mouth. "The caterer. I missed the girls' dress appointments and I need to go to the flower shop to get the centerpieces for the tables." Still wearing yesterday's T-shirt and running shorts, she tossed the blanket aside and swung her bare legs over the side of the bed, the movement causing her to sway a little as a shiver racked her body.

Jake jumped up and cupped her shoulders, guiding her back against the pillows. "You're not going anywhere. You need to be on your antibiotic for a full twenty-four hours before you can even leave this room."

"Don't be ridiculous. I don't have time to lie in bed all day. There's too much to do. And who's going to take care of Annabeth?" Tori's hand flew to her throat as she squeezed her eyes closed while trying to swallow. She reached for her water again.

"And I'll help you get it done. If you don't take care of yourself, Tori, how are you supposed to take care of anyone else, especially Annabeth? And she's with Claudia, by the way."

Tori pressed a hand over her eyes and sighed. "Can I have my computer at least?"

"How about if you rest for a bit longer while I make you some breakfast, then we can go into the family room and do some work together."

"Don't you have chores to do or something?"

"Trying to get rid of me? It's Sunday. Other than milking, it's our only day off."

"Sunday! How long have I been out?"

"Basically since I brought you here yesterday afternoon. Do you remember going to the hospital?"

"Vaguely. I'm sorry you missed church because of me."

"No big deal."

"Really? You think missing church is no big deal?"

"That's not what I meant."

"But that's what you said."

He sighed. "Let me rephrase. I don't mind missing church to take care of you. Okay?"

"That's better." A small smile tugged at the corner of her mouth. More than anything he wanted to lean over and kiss her. But that would do nothing but complicate matters.

Tori dragged a hand through her hair. "I need a shower."

"If you want, I'll have Claudia drop off a change of clothes for you once she gets back."

"I'd like that. Thanks."

"Think you could handle some oatmeal? Or maybe some soup?"

"Either one sounds good."

"Great. I'll make it, and you can rest your throat. I'll come back to get you in a bit."

"Thanks, Jake."

"Anytime."

As he forced himself to walk out of the room and close the door behind him, he realized he meant every word he'd said. He liked taking care of Tori. He liked being there for her to lean on.

She called it rescuing, but he considered it an act of love.

He stalled at the top of the steps and gripped the banister as the truth slammed him in the chest, nearly knocking him off his feet.

He was in love with Tori.

This time he didn't bother trying to deny it. Now he just had to figure out what to do about it.

Two hours later, Jake had reheated Tori's oatmeal after she'd gone back to sleep the first time, then he helped her get settled on the couch with a pillow and afghan.

Freshly showered and bundled in a thick robe despite the eighty-degree temperature outside, Tori clutched her cup of hot tea with honey. "Thanks."

"You're welcome."

She traced one of the stripes on the mug and then looked at him. "Can I ask you a question?"

"Sure."

"What's your relationship with God?"

That was the last question he expected her to ask.

"Where'd that question come from?"

She shrugged. "Something I've been wondering for a while, I guess."

Jake rubbed the back of his neck and turned away from her. He strode to the window, shoved his hands in his pockets and gazed out into the backyard. "I guess it's a bit complicated."

"Sounds like a Facebook status."

"Yeah."

"Why's it complicated?"

"I've been going to church from the time I was born. I've done the whole vacation Bible school, youth group, youth camp thing. I can recite the books of the Bible, memorized Scripture. I figured my ticket was punched to get into Heaven, you know."

He moved away from the window and sat on the end of the coffee table. "But none of that prepared me for the past six years. I lost my wife, my best friend and my mother all within a year. Our farm was nearly destroyed. Then Micah and Evan left and Tucker lost sweet Rayne." He paused and rubbed his forehead. "The hits just kept coming. Man, I was angry. Furious at God for destroying so much. I was doing all the right things, so why was He taking so much from me, from my family? But through it all, I watched Dad and Tucker cling to their faiths. What was wrong with me? Why couldn't I be strong like them?"

"Have you asked how they did it?"

Jake dropped his gaze to his shoes and shook his head. "No. I just figured they were better Christians."

"Jake, you know that's not true. When was the last time you prayed?"

He scoffed. "What's the point? God's got a permanent black check mark in the No column when it comes to answering my prayers."

"That's not true."

"I begged Him to get you to take my calls. I begged Him to save Mom. I'm done. I'm done praying. I'm done begging when He doesn't even care."

"My dad never took us to church. I didn't even own a Bible until college, when one of my roommates invited me to attend a Bible study with her. Then I met you. You were good and kind. You saw me for who I was. You didn't want to change me. Do you remember what you said the night you proposed?"

"Of course. 'You're the one I've been praying for.' And I meant it." He leaned forward and brushed a stray strand of hair off her face.

She grabbed his hand. "You didn't let anyone get in the way of your faith. Not even me. You made me want to be a better person, to want more. We got married, and praying with you each morning before you left for duty…well, those were some of my favorite times together. Then you shipped out. And I was so lonely. Then after I lost the baby and believed the lies my dad told me, I went through my own trial."

"How'd you get through it?"

"I had to make a choice—wallow in the darkness or seek out the Light. I chose the Light. Plus, my boss has this larger-than-life personality, and she wasn't about to let me sink. She was pretty amazing, praying with me, speaking Truth into my life."

"You were lucky to have someone like her in your life."

"It's not about luck, Jake. It's about trusting God even when everything is dark."

"You're doing an awful lot of talking for someone who can barely swallow."

"This is important." She took another sip of tea. "I have another question."

"Shoot."

"Are you seeing someone?" Scarlet rose in her cheeks.

He frowned. "What do you mean?"

"Do you have a new girlfriend?"

"Why would you even ask me that?"

"I saw you with someone. The other day when Claudia and I picked up her wedding dress. You were at Cuppa Josie's with a cute little brunette."

Jake retraced the past couple of days and tried to remember when he'd been in town. Then he smiled and chuckled. "That was Willow, Tucker's sister-in-law. She works with our farm vet. No, I'm not dating her. What gave you that crazy idea?"

Tori picked at the fibers in the blanket. "You seemed very comfortable together. And you had your arm around her."

"She's like a kid sister to me." Jake grinned and leaned closer to brush a kiss above her brow. "Jealous much?"

"No." She scowled at him.

"There's never been another woman in my life since I met you. And that's a promise you can hold on to."

Suddenly Tori's eyes drooped as she sank against the pillow. He took her teacup from her and set it on the table. After tucking the afghan around her shoulders, Jake pressed a kiss to Tori's forehead.

Once she was feeling better and all the chaos died down, they needed to talk about their future, because every time Jake thought about his, Tori was front and center. He hoped she felt the same way, but he didn't want to assume. He wanted to hear the words from her lips.

But he could wait.

For now.

Chapter Eleven

Cracks of thunder ricocheted across the hilltop as flashes of lightning behind the dark, heavy clouds colored the night shades of purple. Pelting rain bulleted the glass. Jake gripped the steering wheel as rain cascading over the truck masked his visibility even with the wipers swiping on high. The whistling wind picked up, grabbing at his vehicle, making it difficult to stay centered in his lane.

A few more minutes and he'd be home.

After being awake since 4:00 a.m., he was ready to hit the sack. The day had been spent with milking, cleaning the barn and getting it ready for the upcoming fund-raiser, baling hay, and then hanging out with Tori for a couple of hours this evening.

He was whipped.

On the plus side, though, their plans for the fund-raiser were falling into place. After it was over, he was going to be writing a lot of thank-you notes. All for a good cause.

If only Micah could be home to participate and see what they had planned for the program. Maybe then he'd see there was hope in his situation and they were there to help—if he would let them.

Another crack of thunder jolted Jake. A jagged dagger of lightning speared the tree line thirty yards to his right.

A quick movement caught his eye. Before he could react, a deer jumped in front of him. He gripped the steering wheel as the front grille took the brunt of the impact.

Thankfully he hadn't been going very fast.

Jake braked, threw on his hazard lights and jumped out of the truck into the pounding rain. The deer appeared dazed. It lay on the asphalt a moment, staggered to its feet, then bounded into the field.

If it hadn't been raining so hard, he might have gone after it to make sure it was okay, but he wouldn't be able to see anything in this weather. A quick glance at his grille showed mainly cosmetic damage, something he could take care of tomorrow, especially with the wind whipping across the fields, forcing branches to bow low and rocking fence posts and lines.

There'd be repairs to be done tomorrow due to the damaging winds.

He hauled himself back into the truck, soaked and shivering in the air-conditioned cab. Minutes later, he swung into the farmhouse driveway and headed inside.

A hot shower, maybe a quick bite to eat, then he could crawl into bed for—a quick glance at his watch showed it being almost midnight—about four hours before starting another day.

Sometimes, for a moment, he wished for a nine-to-five job where he didn't have the scent of manure clinging to him all day long. And he could have somewhat of a normal life instead of worrying about dropping milk prices and rising feed costs, performing backbreaking work that never seemed to end and wondering from year to year what the seasons were going to do to his crops.

Even though farming presented so many challenges, he simply couldn't imagine doing anything else.

After a quick shower, he skipped the food and collapsed on his bed.

He'd barely closed his eyes—or so it seemed—when his alarm went off, dragging him from the dregs of sleep.

After throwing on jeans and a T-shirt, Jake padded quietly down the stairs and through the kitchen to stuff his feet in his barn boots. He stepped onto the back deck and inhaled a lungful of fresh, cool air.

As he crossed the yard, his steps slowed as he glanced across the barnyard.

Something seemed different. Out of place.

But he couldn't figure out what.

Wait a minute…

He strode to the road and headed past the new barn until his feet froze next to the fence.

Goose bumps pebbled his skin as his jaw dropped and his eyes widened. His chest stuttered as he tried to catch a breath that seemed to be lodged in his throat. A chill slicked his skin as his empty stomach rolled.

Gripping each side of his head, he dropped to his knees on the wet grass and stared across the pasture to where the old red barn had collapsed to a pile of splintered, weathered boards around their equipment with the remains of the roof staggered off to the side. Pieces of wood littered the road, pasture and field like firewood.

Destroyed.

Shattered.

Nothing but shambles.

Like his dreams.

His hope.

His heartbeat pounded in his ears as he headed back to the house and stopped outside Dad's bedroom door.

He paused a moment. Was it necessary to wake up Dad at four in the morning? Or could it wait?

What had Dad said? They carried burdens together.

This was one burden he simply couldn't manage on his own. Not even for a couple of hours.

He rapped his knuckles against the panel before turning the handle. "Dad, wake up."

Dad sat up and flicked on the lamp by his bed. "Jake? What's going on? What time is it?"

"A little after four. We've got a problem." Jake crossed his father's bedroom and threw up the pull-down shade.

Rubbing a hand over his face, Dad eased out of bed and headed for the window. He eyes widened as he pressed a hand against the frame.

Jake put a hand on his shoulder. "You okay, Pops?"

Dad nodded, his shoulders sagging as he released a sigh. "Go wake up your brother."

"No need. I'm right here. What's going on?" Tucker stood in the doorway rubbing a fist in his eye.

Jake waved him over to the window and pointed. "Look."

Tucker stood between Jake and Dad, slack-jawed, and groaned. "Not again. When are we going to catch a break?"

Jake stared out the second-story window across the

rooftop of the new barn to the destroyed barn. "I got home at midnight and the barn was fine but the wind had started picking up, too. I never heard a thing after that."

"Neither did I." Dad opened the window and leaned on the sill. Rain droplets clung to the screen as the cool air whisked over them.

"Your wedding's in three days and the fund-raiser's a week later. The auction and barn dance were the main attractions. We're going to have to cancel."

"We're not canceling anything yet. God's not surprised by this, and He's in control. Let's pray first, then figure out where to go from there." Dad put a hand on his and Tucker's shoulders and prayed.

Even though Jake bowed his head, he listened to Dad's words with half an ear. What was the point? Like God was really listening...or even caring about what Dad had to say.

Across the yard, cows bawled from the milk barn.

"The girls are calling, Jake. Do the milking, then we'll figure this out over breakfast." Dad closed the window and reached for his worn Bible resting on his nightstand. "I'm going downstairs to read."

Jake followed Dad out of the room and trudged downstairs. An ache gripped his chest for the hours of planning that had gone into creating an event that would benefit others. And now he just didn't want to think about it.

He dreaded making the call to Tori.

Last night, she'd been excited as she shared how she planned to decorate for the dance. If she wasn't still recovering from strep throat, she would've been alongside him yesterday cleaning the barn.

Now, that was one partnership he could get behind.

A different kind of cleanup would be needed now.

He didn't want to think about the hours of work that needed to be done in only a few days.

He went through the motions of milking. And for a couple of hours, his attention was diverted, but the minute he stepped outside after cleaning the milk barn, the burden of the storm damage weighed on his shoulders.

Outside the farmhouse, he toed off his boots by the back door and headed into the kitchen, only to find Tori at the stove with her back to him. Laughter sounded from the other room.

She turned and smiled, sending a shot of electricity straight to his chest. "Hungry?"

"Famished." He crossed the room and kissed her on the forehead. "What are you doing here?"

She wrapped her arms around him, pressing her cheek to his chest. "Chuck called Claudia and told her about the barn. We came over to see what we could do. I'm so sorry."

"Thanks. You should be resting."

"I'm tired of resting. I'm feeling better than I have in days." She turned and reached for a plate loaded with scrambled eggs and sausage links and handed it to him.

"Thanks." He set it on the table, then filled two cups with coffee. Handing one to her, he nodded toward the table. "Join me?"

She took the cup and smiled. "Sure. Looks like we have to readjust our plans for the fund-raiser."

"More like cancel, don't you think?"

"One little setback and you're ready to give up? Where's your fight, Jake?"

"Curled up in bed, I think." Instead of picking up

his fork, he rested his head in his hand. "I'm tired just thinking of the work that needs to be done."

"Well, good for you, then, because you don't have to do it alone."

He frowned. "What do you mean?"

"Aunt Claudia's been on the phone for the past hour rounding up friends to pitch in and help."

"She can't do that." Jake pushed away from the table, leaving his food untouched.

"Why not?"

"Because—"

"Because you look at asking for help as a sign of weakness. Let me tell you something, Jake—we're all weak. It comes with being human. You can't continue doing everything on your own. Otherwise, you're going to end up broken and worn out. Then what good will you be to your family? You have friends who want to help. Allow them that blessing and stop being so stubborn."

"Hey, I totally get weakness. You think I like doing everything myself? Stopping to ask for help—it's just one more thing to do when I'm trying to take care of everything else that needs to be done. I'm just not used to doing it."

"Now there's a newsflash. Finish your breakfast, pull that fabulous smile you use once in a while out of your pocket and then get ready to lead a crew of people who have no clue what they're doing, but they want to help. And you're going to let them."

Tori moved behind him and rested her hands on his shoulders. "Accept this gift as it's being given and realize there's a lot of strength in working as a team. Stop carrying this farm's burdens on your shoulders, Jake. I have an idea for the fund-raiser, but I can't share it yet. I'm asking you to trust me. Can you do that?"

"Yes, I trust you." He reached for her hand and pressed a kiss into her palm.

"Good. Finish your breakfast. I'm going to work on my idea a bit more."

Instead of picking up his fork, Jake reached for his coffee. He needed the caffeine to keep him going.

Man, he was tired.

His eyes strayed across the table to where Tori had sat briefly in his dad's chair.

Dad's worn black Bible with its cracked leather cover lay open on the table. Jake stretched across the table and picked it up to where it stayed open to Matthew chapter eleven. A familiar verse leaped out at him.

Come unto me, all ye that labour and are heavy laden, and I will give you rest.

He wanted rest for his soul. Longed for someone to share his burdens with. So why did it feel like it was just out of reach?

What would it take to grab hold of that promise? To partner with God, to be yoked with him, to find that rest he longed for?

Tori didn't know if her idea would work but she had to try.

She guided a blindfolded Jake across the barnyard and stopped in front of the closed doors to the new barn. "Wait here a minute. You still trust me?"

"Do I have a choice?"

"Sure you do—you could've removed that blindfold at any time."

"Now you tell me." He shot her that half grin that caused her heart rate to spike.

Tori opened the sliding doors, then hurried back to Jake, taking his hand again, and then led him to the doorway.

"Can I take off this blindfold yet?"

"In a minute." She pressed her hands against his chest. "Listen, I'm going to show you something. If you don't like it, we'll go with plan B. Okay?"

Jake shrugged. "Yeah, sure. Okay."

"Take off your blindfold, but keep an open mind."

Jake snatched the folded blue bandanna off his head and scanned the barn. His jaw dropped as he looked around. "You did this?"

Biting her bottom lip and clasping her hands in front of her, she nodded, still a little uncertain of his reaction.

Jake walked slowly as his eyes scanned the walls and ceiling before settling on her. "This looks…wow."

"Is that a good 'wow'?"

He grinned. "Yes, it's a very good wow. I can't believe the transformation."

Tori released a breath and relaxed her tense body. "This is only a mock-up. The real event will look much better. I just wanted to give you a general idea of what could be done." She pointed to the ceiling. "Instead of those plastic tablecloths I picked up at the dollar store, we'll drape swags of blue and red table rolls from the center beams to the walls. White paper lanterns will hang from the ceiling instead of those cheap balloons. We'll wrap small white Christmassy-type lights around each of the vertical posts going down the center of the room."

She moved to the middle of the room and twirled

with her arms outstretched. "We'll keep half of the space for a dance floor, but we'll add round tables covered with white cloths and chairs. We'll add burlap runners and Mason jar centerpieces done in red, white and blue. Even though the fund-raiser will take place after the Fourth, we can still focus on a patriotic theme."

She grabbed his hand and dragged him over by the door where a pile of weathered boards had been stacked. "Tucker saved these boards from the cleanup crew. I know how much you wanted to use the barn your grandfather had built for the dance, but we can incorporate these boards into the decor along with a couple of old wagon wheels he recovered under the rubble. With strategically placed bales of hay, I think we can still provide that same kind of rustic look you wanted."

"Kind of like mixing the old with the new, huh?"

"Exactly."

She started to share a new thought, but instead she closed her mouth. She needed to stop talking, to allow him time to absorb the proposed changes and respond to her ideas. Maybe even share some of his own.

But the silence made her nervous.

Jake ran his hand over the filthy, beat-up wagon wheel and looked at her with eyes that dug deep into her soul. He brushed his hand on his jeans, then cupped her shoulders, keeping his gaze fixed on her. "When I saw the barn reduced to a pile of rubble, I was ready to give up. Ready to call this whole thing off. But not you. You saw the problem needed a solution, and you reacted, figuring one out. You didn't allow me being a jerk to hold you back. You've been that way from the moment you stormed into the barn, kicked off your heels and offered me an ultimatum. You see what needs to be done, and you dig in to do the work—no matter how smelly or dirty it is. That's a gift, Tori. A real gift. And I'm humbled and thankful to be a recipient of it. You are a real treasure."

To Jake, his words may have been a compliment spoken in the moment only to be forgotten later, but to Tori, his words flowed through her like melted gold, filling in all the cracks and crevices of her heart that had been wrecked and scarred, giving her confidence a foothold to climb toward bigger and better things.

With Sophie's offer in the back of her mind, she couldn't help but wonder if her gift, as Jake called it, was going to be what kept them apart.

The more she worked on the fund-raiser, realizing the depth of her potential—the ability to be the voice for those who lacked the hope or couldn't speak up for themselves—the more she considered Sophie's offer. She had an opportunity to champion others to find solutions, to empower them to rise to the challenges they'd been facing and help them to overcome.

Making that choice could also cost Tori the second chance with Jake she'd desired for years. If she did nothing, though, she could risk losing everything, including herself.

Chapter Twelve

Despite the stormy weather, then three long, hard days of cleanup and repairs on the farm, the morning of Dad and Claudia's wedding dawned clear.

Sunshine turned the morning dew into little glass droplets hanging from freshly cut blades of grass.

Jake stood barefoot on the back deck in shorts and a T-shirt drinking a hot cup of coffee and soaked in the solitude.

In an hour the place would be bustling with activity once Claudia, Tori and Annabeth arrived along with the rest of Claudia's family, even though everyone had stayed late last night to put the finishing touches on the decorations.

Six round tables covered with white cloths and bright pink place mats and pots of flowers sat under a huge tent pitched between the two apple trees in the back-yard. Strings of lights had been twined around the posts and paper lanterns in shades of pink hanging from the center of the canopy bounced in the morning breeze.

Tori planned to bring the rest of the flowers with her.

The thought of seeing her again...well, that warmed him faster than the coffee he'd been sipping.

The back door opened behind him. He turned as Dad stepped onto the deck, holding his mug. "Good morning."

"Hey, Dad."

"It's a great day to get married." Dad clinked his mug against Jake's. "Thank God for second chances."

"Nervous?"

"Nah. More like excited." Dad grinned like Landon did when offered a cookie.

"You deserve it. I'm happy for you. It will be different to have a woman in the house again."

"But the change will be good...for all of us." Dad took another sip of coffee, then set his mug on the deck railing. "What about you? You've been spending a lot more time with Tori lately. By choice, may I add."

"Considering the fund-raiser is next week, we've been working to get everything finished. She's had a lot on her plate, especially with getting sick and the barn being destroyed, so I'm doing what I can to help out."

"Is that the only reason?"

Jake considered his father's question, not wanting to raise false hopes. "I think we're heading into a better place with our relationship."

"It's about time you took charge of your own happiness. She's a sweet girl. Keep the past where it belongs and focus on moving forward. You're both young. Time has a way of granting wisdom, especially through tough life lessons."

He knew that to be true.

"With everything going on, we haven't had time to talk. Really talk."

"Life's always going to be busy, son. Make the time. If she's the one, make her a priority and do what it takes to keep her." Dad clapped him on the shoulder and reached for his mug. "Time to make this old farmer presentable for his bride."

Jake followed Dad into the kitchen, rinsed their mugs and added them to the dishwasher. He headed upstairs to shower.

With Claudia moving in, the farmhouse wouldn't be a bachelor pad any longer. He needed to think about getting his own place so she and Dad could have their privacy.

Problem was, short of building something, houses were in short supply on Holland Hill. And he had no intention of moving into town. He was meant for country living. Plus, there was the perk of rolling out of bed, throwing on clothes and heading to the barn. Leaving the hill wouldn't allow that luxury.

After a quick shower and getting dressed, Jake stood in front of the open window as he buttoned his dress shirt. His gaze traveled across the barnyard and the adjoining pasture and settled on the roof of Tori's house.

Having spent much of his childhood there when his grandparents were alive, Jake was very fond of the place. After Dennis and Claudia moved out, he should've placed an offer on the house. Then the mess of the past few months could've been avoided.

But then he wouldn't have Tori back in his life.

Sure, seeing her at Claudia's that first day had been a shock, but the more time they spent together, the less he liked being apart from her.

And finally admitting the truth to himself had loosened the choke hold of anger that had gripped him since he received those stinkin' divorce papers.

She wasn't the same girl he'd married. But he wasn't the same guy either. Life had a way of maturing them into people who could face challenges together instead of running away when things got tough.

Perhaps Dad was right.

Maybe God had allowed things to happen the way they did to bring them back together. And maybe it was time to step out in faith and lay it all on the line.

What if she didn't feel the same way?

What if he'd been misreading her?

What if he was setting himself up for more heartache?

What if he let fear hold him back and lost the only woman he'd ever loved…again?

Or what if he risked it all and got everything he'd been wanting for so long?

A quiet knock sounded on his door.

He strode barefoot across the room, quickly making work of the last buttons on his shirt, and opened the door to find Tori standing in the doorway wearing a bright pink sleeveless dress that brushed the tops of her knees and matching sandals with sparkly stones that added a couple of inches to her height. Her hair had been gathered in a side ponytail of curls that fell in front of her left shoulder. Cream and pink flowers had been pinned in her hair, the petals brushing her jaw.

He swallowed…more like gulped. "You look…amazing."

A blush brightened her cheeks. "Thank you. You look dashing yourself."

Jake glanced down at his untucked shirt opened at the throat and bare feet. "I'm not quite ready."

"Doesn't matter." Her eyes roamed the length of him, then she gave him a coy smile. "You still look good. Sorry to interrupt but I need your help stashing my wedding present for Chuck and Claudia."

"Sure, give me a minute to put on my socks and shoes, and I'll give you a hand."

"No need." Tori turned away from the door and beckoned.

Jake grabbed his dress socks he'd tossed on his unmade bed. Then pulled the comforter up to the pillows in some semblance of order.

"Hey, big brother."

Jake's heart stuttered.

That voice…

He whipped around to find Evan…and Micah standing inside his bedroom.

His socks fell from his fingers. "What? How…?"

He walked toward them slowly and stretched out a hand, almost afraid to touch them for fear their presence wouldn't be real.

Evan snagged his hand and jerked Jake to him, wrapping him in a tight one-armed hug.

Jake's heart picked up speed as his chest shuddered. He squeezed his eyes against the rush of tears and tried to swallow past the knot in his throat. He wrapped an arm around Micah's neck and pulled his baby brother into a hug.

Over their shoulders, his damp eyes tangled with Tori's. He mouthed, "Thank you."

She smiled, blew him a flirty kiss, then brushed

away her own stray tear as she backed out of the room and closed the door.

He released his brothers and rubbed his eyes.

"Getting soft on us, bro?"

"Allergy season. What are you doing here? I mean, how did you get here? How did Tori pull this off?"

"She's one amazing girl." Evan, never one to sit still, prowled around Jake's room. He grabbed a quarter from the mug of change Jake kept on his dresser and rolled the coin between his fingers. "She called a few weeks ago and asked for my help in reaching out to Micah."

"I just talked to you the other day. You didn't mention it."

"She asked me not to. Said she wanted to surprise you, too. And she didn't want to let you down again if it didn't work out. Interesting choice of words, if you ask me. She's the one you talked about, isn't she?"

Jake glanced at the time and snapped his dress watch on his wrist, then tucked in his shirt. "Yes, she's the one."

"She's hot."

"Back off." Jake shot Evan a dirty look as he sat on the edge of the bed and pulled on his socks.

Evan held up his hands. "No worries. I don't take what's not mine."

Jake shoved his feet in his dress shoes, tied them quickly, then looked at Micah, who hadn't said a word since entering his room. He stayed close to the door with his back pressed against the frame. His right sleeve hung limply at his side.

Etched lines had aged him, chasing away the boyish looks. His long hair had been cut but his dark beard couldn't disguise the puckered scarring on the right side of his face.

"Micah, it's good to see you, man. So good."

"Yeah, you, too."

More than anything Jake wanted to rewind time and go back to that night he'd fought with his brother, calling him irresponsible and reckless. "Listen..." His words trailed off. How did he even begin to apologize?

"Yeah, me, too."

"We good?"

"Sure, why not?"

Someone rapped on the door, causing Micah to jump away from the frame. His eyes darted around the room as he crouched and raised his left hand into a fist.

Evan rested a hand on Micah's shoulder. "Relax, man. You're safe. It's just someone at the door."

Micah's face blazed as he pushed to his feet.

Jake opened the door and found Tori again. "Chuck and Claudia are waiting in the living room wearing blindfolds. I said their surprise was too big for me to carry so I needed Jake's help."

"Where's Tuck? Does he know they're here?"

She nodded. "He picked them up from the airport last night. They stayed at my place."

"They were just down the road?"

"Don't be mad. Their flights were delayed so they got in late."

Jake traced the frame of her face and smiled down at her. "I'm not mad."

She reached for his hand and squeezed. "Good. Let's get on with the surprise so Aunt C can finish getting ready. I have a feeling she's going to need to repair her makeup."

He followed Evan and Micah out of the room and reached for Tori's hand. "I know you did this for Dad and Claudia, and two little words seem so insignificant, but thank you. I don't know how you pulled this off, but I will never forget this."

Tori's smile widened. "Maybe we can find a quiet moment later to, you know, talk? Then I can tell you all about it."

He threaded his fingers through hers. "I'd like that. There are some things I need to say."

As she walked beside him down the hall, her small hand enveloped in his, Jake realized Dad's life wasn't the only one changing today.

Tori had done the impossible—bringing his family back together. He couldn't ever repay her for such an incredible gift, but he could start by offering her a second chance at a new future together.

Dad was right—he needed to take charge of his own happiness, and that was going to happen today.

Tori wanted nothing more than to grab a pink lemonade cupcake, refill her coffee and find a quiet corner where she could catch her breath.

Scratch that. She wanted to close her eyes for a few minutes, then she'd eat her cupcake and drink her coffee in peace.

But that wasn't going to happen anytime soon.

So she'd settle for grabbing a cupcake and finding a quiet spot to enjoy it.

Around her, music and laughter flowed like iced tea on a hot summer's day. The scent of barbecue drifted down the table from where the catering staff was taking care of the leftovers.

The wedding had been beautiful. Both of Claudia's sons had walked her down the aisle between rows of white chairs to where Chuck stood under the arch of apple tree branches. Tori, Claudia's two daughters-in-law and Annabeth, all wearing different shades of pink, stood beside her as bridesmaids while Jake, Tucker, Evan and Micah stood with their dad. Olivia and Landon stole the show as flower girl and ring bearer as they elbowed each other to be the first ones down the aisle.

While Chuck and Claudia said their vows, Tori's gaze tangled with Jake's as she remembered reciting similar ones to him. Did he remember their tiny wedding at that little chapel nestled in the vineyard with the stained glass windows where they'd promised to love and cherish for as long as they both lived?

The country band Claudia and Chuck had chosen broke into a well-known line dance number, jerking her away from the memory. Ladies dressed in sundresses and skirts kicked off their heels and lined up next to men in jeans and dress shirts. They stomped, clapped and moved their feet in unison with a lot more rhythm and coordination than she had.

Tucker and Evan danced on each side of Claudia while Micah reclined next to Chuck, watching them. Annabeth stood on the tops of Jake's feet as he held her tiny hands and danced in slow circles. She grinned up at him, and the look of love on his face about melted Tori's heart. He lifted her in his arms, and she pressed a kiss to his cheek, then rested her head on his shoulder. Jake caught her eye and a slow smile spread across his face. Once the song ended, Annabeth twisted out of his arms and ran off to catch up with Olivia and Landon.

Jake refilled his iced tea, then wandered over to her.

He rested a hand on the back of her chair. "Have I thanked you for what you've done for Dad and Claudia today?"

"About a dozen times."

"Let's make it a dozen and one, then. Thanks again for what you've done to bring our family back together. And for this party. If the fund-raiser is even a quarter good as this, then we're golden."

She lifted her chin, pulled up her shoulders and shot him a knowing look. About time he realized her abilities. "They're two different events. This is a celebration. The other is to raise awareness and to gain donors to partner with your program."

"Even so, it's all happening because of you. You make things happen. It's your superpower."

"Does that mean I get a cape and some sort of high-tech signal to flash in the sky when my services are needed?"

"Some of the best superheroes don't wear capes. When people tell me what a great party this is, I've been singing your praises."

"That's so sweet. I don't know what to say except thank you."

"Once the fund-raiser is over, I can pretty much guarantee your business calendar will be booked."

Tori looked away. She needed to tell him about Sophie's offer and the numerous texts that followed. But not now. Not here. And not today.

Today was about celebrating family.

So when?

She toyed with the fluted wrapper on the cupcake. Her decision depended on many things. Even though she was still living out of boxes, she had a house of her own that she loved. Annabeth had a yard where she could run and play. She loved being close to her aunt. And then there was Jake.

"Hey, you okay?" Jake bumped her shoulder lightly with his.

"What?" She looked up at him.

"I've been talking and realized you weren't paying attention. Are you feeling okay?" The look of concern on his face nearly had her spilling everything.

She smothered a yawn she didn't have to fake and waved away his words. "A little tired but I'm fine. Don't worry about me."

Jake shoved his hands in his pockets and kicked at the grass with the toe of his dress shoe. A frown lined his forehead, then he looked at her. "I know this isn't the best time or the right place, Tori, but the more I'm around you, the more I like worrying about you. I *want* to worry about you. Know what I'm saying?"

Tori's heart quickened. She didn't want to assume, but was Jake saying what she'd been waiting to hear?

She glanced down at the somewhat mangled cupcake in her hands. Pink frosting clung to her fingers. She set the dessert on the table and reached for a napkin.

"By your silence, I'm guessing you don't." A scowl laced his face as he downed the rest of his drink.

She focused on her sticky fingers and shook her head. "No, it's not that. You just caught me off guard. We do need to talk. I have things I need to say but today's not the time. Focus on your family. I'm not going anywhere."

A grin replaced his scowl. He leaned over and wrapped his arms around her.

She clung to his broad shoulders, soaking in the security of his embrace, and breathed in the scent of his soap.

Jake brushed his lips over her ear, his breath warm against her skin. "Dance with me."

She nodded, not trusting her voice. He took her hand, guided her through the maze of tables and pulled her into his arms. They fit together perfectly, as if the pairing had been decided long before either of them had been born.

As he drew her closer, she rested her cheek against his chest, his heartbeat a steady sound in her ear. His chin grazed the top of her head as they danced to a country ballad about eyes meeting.

Jake lowered his head and sang along, his voice for her ears only.

Closing her eyes, she breathed a sigh and committed to memory every move, every sound, every nuance that would remind her of this unforgettable moment.

The song ended but Jake was slow to release her. She turned her face up to look at him. He traced a finger down her cheekbone and across her jaw. He brushed a gentle kiss across her lips. Then he pulled her closer to his chest. "We need to talk. And soon. Lady, you're driving me crazy."

In a good way, she hoped.

Tears pricked her eyes. Finally, things were beginning to fall into place.

So why was she feeling so unsettled?

Chapter Thirteen

It couldn't be morning already.

Seemed like Tori had just crawled into bed.

Stifling a groan, she squinted against the light streaming through the crack in the curtains and buried her head under her pillow. She patted her nightstand for her phone to check the time.

9:00 a.m.!

She'd slept way later than expected. They were going to be late for church.

Where was Annabeth?

Why hadn't she woken her? Or Poppy, needing to go outside?

Tori tossed the summer quilt aside as a crash sounded from the kitchen followed by an "Oh, no!"

She grabbed her phone and hurried out of her room. She rushed down the stairs and into the kitchen to find Annabeth wearing her Peppa Pig pajamas and standing in a growing puddle of milk with Poppy beside her lapping the milk quickly before it could be cleaned up.

Annabeth looked at her with wide eyes brimming

with tears. "Sorry, Aunt Tori. I wanted to make you breaffast. I dropped the milk."

Tori scooped her up and set her on the stool at the breakfast bar. "You sit here and I'll clean up the mess."

"Am I in time-out?"

"What? No, honey. I just want to clean up the milk so you don't slip and fall. I'd feel sad if you got hurt." She picked up the leaking jug and set it in the sink. Then she grabbed several dish towels to mop up the liquid.

As she dropped dripping towels in the sink, the doorbell rang, sending Poppy into a barking fit. Milky footprints stamped the floor as the dog raced across the room and headed for the door. Her phone chimed from the breakfast bar.

Tori ignored it and dried her hands on the way to the door. Poppy danced around her feet, nearly tripping her. She whipped it open to find Jake standing on her welcome mat. Dressed in a light blue untucked buttondown shirt, gray shorts and black leather flip-flops, he held a bouquet of white daisies with baby's breath wrapped in yellow tissue paper and a Cuppa Josie's bag.

Poppy jumped up on his legs, begging for attention.

"Hey." She ran a hand over her tangled mess of hair and tried to use the door to shield the fact she was still in pajama pants and a tank top.

Jake grinned and held up the bag. "Good morning. I brought you something. And stopped to see if you wanted to ride to church with me."

"What is it?" Her mouth watered as she smelled cinnamon and sugar.

"Let me in, and I'll tell you."

"Oh, yeah, sorry. It's just a little crazy at the moment. My brain is like applesauce this morning. Not the sweet kind, but the mushy, left-out-on-the-counter-resembling-a-science-project kind."

And now she was babbling like an idiot.

"Everything okay?"

"Yes. Mostly. I overslept. Annabeth tried to fix me breakfast and spilled the milk. I was cleaning that up and trying to keep Poppy out of it when my phone rang the same time you came to the door, which sent Poppy into a barking spasm." She scooped up her dog and opened the door wider, waving for him to enter. "Welcome to the chaos."

As they headed to the kitchen, she could hear talking and found Annabeth with Tori's phone pressed to her ear.

"Who are you talking to, honey?"

"Mommy." She grinned, exposing the vacant area where her tooth had been.

Kendra must've been the one who called while Tori hurried to answer the door. "May I talk to Mommy, please?"

Annabeth held up a finger—something she'd seen Tori do many times.

Tori turned on her Keurig and pulled two white mugs out of the cabinet. "Want some coffee?"

"Sure, they'll go great with the cinnamon rolls I brought." He leaned on the counter and glanced at her, then jerked his gaze away.

She looked down to find her shirt had ridden up, exposing a couple of inches of her waist. She set the cups on the counter. "Excuse me a minute."

She hurried to her room, exchanging her pajamas for a red-and-white-striped T-shirt dress, and yanked a brush through her hair before pulling it back into a ponytail. With no time for makeup, it would have to do.

She reentered the kitchen to find Jake mopping the drying puddle of milk by the fridge. He'd placed the flowers in a drinking glass filled with water. Annabeth walked slowly across the room and held the phone out to Tori. Her bottom lip puffed out. "Mommy wants to say hi."

Tori took the phone and gave a quick hug to Annabeth, who always hated saying goodbye when Kendra called—not that Tori could blame her. "Hey, you. What's up?"

"I have only a couple of minutes left to talk. I was getting worried when you didn't answer my other calls."

"Sorry. I overslept and didn't hear my phone ring, then a bunch of things happened at once."

"Listen, Tor. I didn't want to get into this over the phone, especially since I don't have much time left, but my orders changed. I'm returning stateside. I'm coming home."

"That's great. When?"

"Could be as early as next week."

"Wow, I didn't think the military moved that quickly."

"This has been in the works for a while." Kendra paused. "Thing is, I reenlisted and I've picked up staff sergeant. I've received my first request for my next duty station."

"Congrats! That's fantastic. Where are you headed?"

"California."

Tori dropped on one of the breakfast bar stools. "California? Wow, that's quite a distance from Pennsylvania. And isn't that where…" Her voice trailed off.

"Yes, it's where Matthew lives."

"Oh, Kendra, please tell me you're not—" Tori curled her nails into her palm.

"I don't want to get into this now." Kendra used the same placating tone Tori had heard when Annabeth threw a fit.

Tori schooled her voice. "He walked out on you. And Annabeth."

"He's changed and wants a second chance. We've been talking for a while."

Tori paced in front of the breakfast bar, throwing a hand in the air. "How can you trust him after the pain he's caused?"

"Probably the same way you're asking Jake to trust you again for a second chance." Kendra's words hit so hard that Tori rubbed her chest with her fist. "I gotta go, sis. Hug Annabeth for me. Love you."

The line went silent as Kendra's parting words slid like ice through Tori's veins. She dropped the phone on the counter and buried her face in her hands.

Jake rested a hand on her back between her shoulder blades. "Everything okay?"

She shook her head.

Jake turned her gently and wrapped her in his arms. "Anything I can do?"

Her arms slid around his waist. "You're doing it."

His embrace offered her everything she'd always wanted—security and a sense of belonging.

Jake kissed the top of her head, then tilted her chin for her eyes to meet his. "Talk to me. What's going on?"

Tori pulled away and moved to the sink, where she rinsed out the milk-soaked dish towels. "My sister is returning stateside. She's reenlisted and has been promoted to staff sergeant."

"Congrats to her. Where's she headed?"

"California."

"California? What does that mean for you?"

"I don't know. Kendra said she might be home as early as next week. Said we'd talk then."

"What does that mean for the fund-raiser? The house you've worked so hard on?" He paused and cleared his throat. "Us?"

Tori slapped the last towel in the sink, spraying milk across the counter, and whirled around. "I don't know."

She wanted to scream and stomp her feet and kick something, but she couldn't do any of those. She dug her fingernails into her palms again and blinked back the wetness blurring her vision. "Annabeth's father lives in California and is back in the picture. Kendra was devastated when Matthew walked out on them. I moved in to help care for Annabeth while Kendra had duty. When she received orders for overseas, she granted me temporary custody to care for Annabeth. We moved back to Pittsburgh and then ended up here after my dad died."

Her chest heaved as her voice rose. She waved a hand around the room. "So now I have a choice to make—leave everything I've been working toward here in Shelby Lake and be close to my family or stay here and leave my family behind. No matter what I choose, my heart is going to break. I just can't believe he has the nerve to contact her again after what he'd done."

"Your sister is a grown woman who can make her own choices. I'm sure she's given this a lot of thought."

"What if he hurts her again?" She gripped the edge of the breakfast bar and lifted her eyes to him.

Jake scrubbed a hand across the back of his neck. "I've been asking myself that same question."

Tori felt the color drain from her face. "You don't trust me. Even after everything I've done to prove to you that I've changed, you're still waiting for me to walk away again, aren't you?"

"Tori…" He held up a hand.

She smacked it away. "I don't know what else I can do to earn your love, Jake, but I'm done trying. I will finish what I started with the fund-raiser, then I'll be out of your life for good. No more wondering. I'll make it easier for you." She brushed her hands together, then tossed them in the air.

"Easier? Tori, would you let me—"

"I have a million things to do today but first I need to check on Annabeth. You can see yourself out. We won't be making it to church today."

Tori hurried out of the kitchen before she made a bigger fool of herself and headed for the living room, where some educational program blared from the TV.

She wanted nothing more than to head upstairs and turn back time. She needed a do-over because in the hour she'd been awake, her life had fallen apart and she had no idea how to piece it back together.

How had everything fallen apart so quickly?

Jake had knocked on Tori's door hoping to talk and ended up losing everything…again.

In the days since their fight—was it even a fight if he wasn't given a chance to share his side?—Tori had resorted to clipped texts and brief emails to communicate with him about the fund-raiser.

But all of her hard work was paying off.

Holland Hill hadn't seen this much traffic since the tornado. The cloudless blue sky with the gentle breeze had people wanting to be outside. And what better place than on a farm.

Smoke billowed from the industrial-sized grills sizzling with chicken and ribs Lena and her husband had set up and manned. People gathered under the oversize tents set up where the old barn had been to eat barbecue, fresh sweet corn, baked beans and apple pie made from Dad's own apple orchards.

Red, white and blue balloons tied on fence posts bobbed and weaved in the breeze that swept across the green fields.

Chatter and laughter blended with the clomping of Westley's and Buttercup's hooves as they pulled the hay wagon full of people. Baaing and bleating sounded from the lambs and miniature goats on loan from the Matthews farm in the front pasture petting area.

The country band that had played at Dad and Claudia's wedding set up in the new barn, prepping for tonight's barn dance as the auctioneer's fast talking and consistent rapping of his gavel proved the community donations were bringing in money for the project. A cornhole tournament had been set up in the side yard between the farmhouse and barns.

Being an introvert, Jake did what he could to avoid crowds, but today, he had to be front and center taking his turn under the information canopy to share the program's vision and to answer questions, ensuring visitors were having a good time. All he wanted to do was retreat to the creek and lick his wounds.

The more he ran their conversation over in his head, the more annoyed he'd become. Tori hadn't even given him time to explain his remark. If she had, he would have assured her he had moved past that way of think-

ing. Instead she jumped to conclusions and did everything she could to avoid him today.

Maybe she had the right idea. Maybe this relationship
was more trouble than it was worth. She could leave
and he could go back to tending the farm. Let things
go back to the way they were.

But he didn't want that anymore.

She was his last thought before his head hit the pillow
and his first thought upon waking. He wanted her beside
him. As his wife. His partner. He wanted to start a family with her. He wanted to grow old together and create
a legacy that could be passed down to their children.

But that wasn't going to happen if he couldn't talk
to her.

"Hey, brother, looks like your fund-raiser's a smash-
ing success." Tucker dropped in the empty chair behind the table and clinked his cup of lemonade against
Jake's iced tea.

"Thanks to Tori's hard work."

"Seems like you guys made a great team. Where is
she anyway? I figured you two would be hanging out
together."

"She's busy making sure everything's running
smoothly."

Tuck watched the crowds, then faced him. "You
know, Jake, I don't say this often enough, but thank
you."

"For what?"

"For being you. When you see a need, you fill it.
Working the farm may not have been your life's ambi-
tion, but you've taken over after Dad got hurt to keep it
going. After Rayne died, you stepped in to help with the

twins. You're doing right by Leo and Micah by starting this project. I'm proud of you, man."

"You growing soft on me, Tuck?"

He laughed. "Don't worry—that's not going to happen. You've inspired me to make some changes, too."

"Yeah, like what?"

He drained his lemonade, then set the empty cup on the table. "I'm going back to school to get my degree in grief counseling. Sadly, I'm way too familiar with the topic. If I can help others get through it, then that's a good thing, right? With Dad and Claudia married, the twins starting kindergarten in the fall, I want to be a hands-on dad. Not a jaded, worn-out wreck who survives on caffeine. I've been hiding behind my paramedic uniform since Rayne died because I failed at saving my own wife, so maybe I could save someone else, you know?"

"Her death was a freaky accident, man. You know that, right?"

Tuck balanced his elbows on his knees and steepled his fingers. "I do, but a day doesn't go by without me missing her. And though it's going to be tough, it's time for the kids and me to move back to our own place. Our crashing at the farmhouse was supposed to be temporary. Dad and C need their own space without the kids underfoot all the time."

"Don't suppose you'd want to rent out a room?" Even asking that question made Jake's heart sink deeper in his chest.

Tuck shot him a puzzled look. "What about you and Tori? I figured you'd be making plans to be with her."

"Yeah, that's not going to happen. Somehow I put my foot in my mouth."

"What'd you do?"

Jake shook his head. "I have no idea."

"Ask her."

"She's avoiding me."

"You two…" Tucker chuckled and shook his head. "And people wonder why I don't want to date."

Jake clapped his brother on the back. "Stay single, man. It's so much easier."

"Says the bachelor moping over a girl."

"I'm not moping."

"Then go talk to her."

"And if she doesn't want to listen?"

Tuck rolled his eyes. "Do I have to tell you everything? If there are two things I've learned about women, it's they want to be valued and to be heard. Tell her how you feel. Do whatever it takes to make her listen. If you're willing to let her go without a fight, then you're a fool who doesn't deserve her anyway."

Jake downed the rest of his watered-down tea and pushed to his feet. "If this goes wrong…"

"Way to go, Mr. Positivity."

Jake shook his head and strode across the yard to find Tori. Maybe she was in the barn watching the auction.

He found her standing in a corner of the barn talking to a woman who appeared as out of place on the farm as he did in the city. The woman was dressed in a red blouse, black flowy pants, a long sheer gray jacket and crazy high heels on her feet, and her streaked dark hair had been twisted in some kind of fancy knot on her head.

As he headed toward them, his gaze caught Tori's and she gave him a startled deer-in-the-headlights look as she jerked her eyes back to the woman. What were they talking about? She slid a cool smile in place. "Jake."

"Hey, Tori. Who's your friend?"

"Sophie, this is Jake Holland. His family owns this farm." She glanced at Jake. "This is Sophie Mays, my former boss."

Jake extended his hand. "Pleasure to meet you, ma'am."

She shook his hand but didn't release it as her eyes looked him over. "Well, now, aren't you a tall drink of water."

"Welcome to Holland Family Farm. Please let us know if we can help you with anything."

"You could convince this young lady to consider my offer."

Jake caught the subtle shake of her head Tori had given Sophie. Why? What was going on?

Tori's eyes widened as she cleared her throat. "Sophie, I…uh…haven't had a chance to talk to Jake about anything yet. We've been so busy with getting ready for the fund-raiser and all."

Sophie tapped her lips with a manicured finger. "So you're the one Tori's been talking about. I hope my faux pas doesn't cause any trouble."

"What's going on?" He touched Tori's elbow. "Do you have a minute?"

She shifted slightly so her arm was out of his touch. "Can it wait? Sophie just arrived from Pittsburgh, and I don't want to be rude."

Jake shoved his fingers in the front pockets of his cargo shorts and ground his jaw. "Sure thing. Whatever." He nodded to Sophie. "Nice meeting you. Thank you for coming to the fund-raiser."

"My late husband was former military. Career navy. Twenty years. This is a program I'd love to support in his name. Do you have information I could review?"

"Yes, ma'am." Jake pulled one of the program brochures out of his back pocket and handed it to her. "This offers information about the program, including the link to our secure website where you can make donations or sign up as a monthly sponsor."

Sophie took the brochure and slid the glasses hanging from a beaded chain around her neck onto her nose. "Thank you. I think I will refill my lemonade and look this over. Tori, darling, I'll catch up with you in a bit. Jake, I'm sure I'll see you soon." She breezed out of the barn, leaving behind a trail of expensive perfume.

Jake leaned a shoulder against the wall. "What was that about?"

"What was what about?" She crossed her arms over her chest.

"Come on, Tori. Stop playing games."

Several people gathered for the auction glanced in their direction at Jake's raised voice.

Tori shot him a desperate look, then slid a smile in place. "Shh, keep your voice down."

"I haven't seen you in a few days. You're ignoring me, and I want to know why."

Tori waved a hand around the barn. "Take a look around, Jake. I've been a little busy finishing up details about the fund-raiser. My sister's flying in tonight. She and Annabeth are flying to California early tomorrow. I've been trying to get her ready to go. And I haven't ignored you. I've responded to your texts and emails."

"It's not the same." He rubbed a thumb over her cheek. "I've missed you."

Tori caught his hand and moved it away from her face. "Don't. Please. I can't do this."

"What's going on, Tori? What was Sophie talking about?"

"Can we talk about this later?"

"No, you keep putting me off, and it's twisting me in knots."

Tori bit her bottom lip as she lowered her gaze and picked at the side of her thumb. She lifted her face, and tears shimmered in her eyes. "I'm leaving Shelby Lake, Jake."

Those five words punched him in the gut, stealing his breath. He swallowed. Hard. "What do you mean you're leaving? What are you talking about?"

"Kendra called the other day and said she doesn't want me to go to California with her and Annabeth. She and Matthew are reconciling and want to start fresh as a family. I've been crying for three days. Staying here in Shelby Lake…it's just not going to work. I was fooling myself in thinking I'd be enough for you." Tori drew in a shuddering breath. "Sophie offered me partnership in her PR company, and I'm going to take it."

"You've decided all of this and I don't get a say?"

"It's my life, Jake. And as you reminded me weeks ago, I'm not your wife. I don't belong here, remember? I'm nothing but a distraction to you."

"Sure, maybe at first, but things have changed. I've changed. You've changed."

She shook her head. "But I haven't. I still want the same things. I want to be with someone who loves me. Who values me. Who wants to be distracted by me. I want to be someone's first priority. And I don't feel that with you."

"You're not being fair. You've made up your mind without even hearing what I have to say. You shut me out. I do love you, Tori, and I want to make this work, but the minute things get tough, you run." He grabbed her hand. "Stay. Here with me. Let's work this out."

"Leave the farm and come with me."

"And do what? My life is on the farm. It's all I know."

"Learn something new."

"What about the Fatigues to Farming program? I can't walk away from that."

"But you can walk away from me? Aren't your dad and brothers a part of it, too?"

"All of these people here today are supporting us. And the veterans like Leo and Micah—where will their hope come from?"

"God. Jake, you're trying to atone for something that was beyond your control. You want to fix something only God can do."

"Don't be ridiculous."

"You go through the motions but the truth is you're so angry at God for the past six years that it's clouding your thinking. You shut Him out and try to do things on your own. When was the last time you prayed? Real, authentic, transparent prayers? You keep saying you want to offer hope to these veterans, but what about hope for yourself?"

"Tori, you're asking the impossible."

"I'm not. And deep down, you know it. You're the one who's afraid of letting go, afraid of releasing some of that responsibility you cling to like a life vest. You need to learn to trust God enough to carry your burdens for you. Otherwise, you're going to lead a very lonely life." Without another word, Tori walked out of the barn.

Jake strode after her, but Evan headed in his direction. "Dude, you gotta come. It's Micah. He's getting ready to split."

He gazed after Tori, then bounced back to Evan, who waited for him to follow. Jake heaved a sigh and headed into the farmhouse, where Micah headed down the stairs with a duffel on his left shoulder.

"Hey, man. Where you going?"

"I gotta head out, man. Something's come up." Micah edged closer to the door.

"You were going to leave without saying goodbye? What about Dad? What about this? We did this for you." Jake's voice rose.

Micah gripped his bag and looked at Jake, his eyes glinting like steel. "No, brother, you did it for you. Look, man, I respect what you're doing and all, but it's not my scene. I never wanted to be a farmer. That was your gig. I have other plans."

"Like which park bench to sleep on?"

Micah scoffed. "You don't know anything about me."

"Whose fault is that?"

"Everything's black-and-white with you, isn't it? Things aren't always as they seem, Jake." Micah reached for the front doorknob.

"At least tell Dad goodbye."

Micah lowered his head, and for a moment Jake thought he'd turn, drop his bag and stay. Instead he turned the handle and opened the door. "It's better this way. For everyone."

"How can you be so selfish?" Jake palmed the door and pushed it closed.

"Are you serious? I sacrificed my family, my body, and nearly lost my life to fight a war I didn't even believe in. You called me reckless and irresponsible, but where were you when I was in that hospital bed? Where were your cards? Your phone calls?"

"You made it clear you wanted nothing to do with me when everyone but me was invited to your boot camp graduation. I stayed behind to run the farm—to keep our family legacy going."

"No, you stayed where it was safe, Jake. I looked up to you, but when we lost Mom, you expected everyone to grieve like you, to do everything the way you did. Guess what, man? It ain't happening. I'll live my life as I choose and you have no say about it. Learn to take some risks, Jake, before you lose everything you love. Now get out of my way." Micah shoved him aside, yanked open the door and walked out, slamming it so hard the front window rattled.

Risks?

Was he crazy?

Farming was a daily risk, but he needed to be responsible—to preserve the family legacy, to offer hope to those who needed it.

Jake stormed out the back door and headed for the milk barn, the one place where he could be alone. He shoved through the swinging door and sat on the steps leading to the pit. Hadn't he just told Tori he loved her? But that wasn't enough. She was leaving anyway.

Taking risks led to heartbreak. And he had endured enough to last a lifetime.

Chapter Fourteen

Tonight was supposed to be a night of celebration.

With the help of the Holland family and a whole lotta prayer, the fund-raiser brought in more revenue than they'd expected, along with monthly sponsors for continued success.

With Kendra returning stateside, Sophie leaving the city to convince her in person to take the partnership position and her fight with Jake, Tori's emotions swirled inside her.

She'd come to Shelby Lake looking for a fresh start, but it looked like she'd be starting all over again elsewhere.

She couldn't stay here. Being neighbors with Jake would be impossible. Not when she wanted more. Needed more than what he was willing to give.

For once she wanted someone to put her first, and if that made her selfish, then so be it.

The look on Jake's face when she asked if he'd be willing to leave the farm to be with her...well, that cemented her thinking.

The guy lived and breathed the farm. She would

never be a priority. Maybe it wasn't the right time or place to have the conversation, but before she gave Sophie her final answer, Tori needed to know where she stood with him.

He'd made it clear—his life was on the farm, and she could join him there or be on her way. Thing was, she'd grown to love the farm, and Jake had finally said the words she'd longed to hear.

But it wasn't enough. Not now. Not anymore.

Someone knocked lightly on her door.

Her heart leaped.

Jake?

She blew out an unsteady breath to settle her pounding heartbeat. She opened it and found Aunt Claudia on the other side. She swallowed her disappointment and pasted a smile in place.

"Hey, what's up?"

"I know it's late, but I wanted to let you know again how proud I am of you and what you've done for the Holland family. Chuck's just beaming. You've given them a great gift, sweetheart."

"Thanks, Aunt C. It's a worthy cause and I was happy to help. Come in. I was about to make some tea. Want some?"

"Yes, please. That sounds great. Something herbal if you have it."

Tori pulled two mugs out of the cabinet and set them on the counter, then reached for a basket of assorted tea bags and handed them to Claudia. "Take your pick."

Claudia unwrapped a peppermint tea bag, placed it in her cup, then handed it to Tori, who filled it with hot water from the Keurig. "I'm sorry if I'm out of line, but you didn't seem happy today. What's going on?"

Tori clutched the edge of the counter and lowered her chin to her chest. "Life's been a bit complicated lately."

"Want to talk about it?" Tori handed Claudia's tea to her, then made her own cup. She led the way into the living room. They sat on the couch facing each other and Tori told her everything.

"With Kendra and Annabeth leaving in the morning, and you and Chuck going on your honeymoon, I just don't feel like I belong here anymore. Every room in this house reminds me of Jake or Annabeth. Maybe it would be best to find my fresh start elsewhere." Her vision blurred. Tori closed her eyes, but a lone tear managed to slip down her face.

"Oh, honey." Claudia wrapped an arm around her shoulders and pulled her close. "I thought Jake said he loved you."

"He did. But they're just words. Is it wrong for me to want some action to back them up? He'll never leave the farm."

"Do you feel it was fair to ask him to?"

Poppy put her paws on Tori's leg, wanting to be picked up. Tori lifted the dog and stroked her. "I'm not sure. All my life I did everything to please other people. And now Sophie offers me this incredible opportunity at the same time Jake decides he's ready to move forward with us. With Kendra taking Annabeth all the way to California, I just feel… I don't know, it's time to live my life on my terms. I just don't know where I belong."

"You're a child of God. You'll always belong with Him. If you feel the new job is where God is leading you, then you should go. But if you're using it as an excuse to run away, then maybe you're going for the wrong reasons."

"By partnering with Sophie, I can give back and raise awareness for voices that struggle to be heard."

"Why do you feel you have to move to Pittsburgh to do that?"

"That's where Sophie's office is."

"With computers and today's technology, you could work almost anywhere. I know I'm being selfish, but I'd hate to see you leave when I've just gotten to know you again. Promise me you will pray about your choices."

"I promise."

Aunt Claudia glanced at her watch and stood. "I need to get back before Chuck worries. We're leaving first thing in the morning. I hope to see you when I get back."

"You will. No matter where I am." Tori gave her a hug. "Have a great time in Charleston. I heard it's beautiful there."

"One of my favorite cities."

Tori walked her aunt to the door, then shut it behind her.

God, what do I do about Jake? This house? The job?
Silence reigned.

The past two months filled her heart with memories she'd cherish forever. The good and the not so good.

A tear slid down her cheek and she wiped it away with her finger as she headed for the stairs. Tomorrow was going to be a life-changing day. She loved caring for her niece. Not having her close by was going to be so tough, but Annabeth needed to be with her parents, no matter how much it broke Tori's heart.

Even though she didn't want to, she needed to talk to Jake.

But that would have to wait until morning.

The emotions of the past few days had caught up

with her and she wanted nothing more than sleep. Perhaps in the morning, her choices would be made clear. No matter what happened, someone was going to end up hurt. And there was nothing she could do to fix it.

Tori refused to take the cowardly way out again. This time she'd tell Jake to his face why she was leaving. No matter how badly she wanted to, she wouldn't hide behind a letter.

She'd hoped a good night's sleep would have given her clarity about the right decision to make. Despite her fatigue, she'd tossed and turned, finally getting out of bed at 5:00 a.m. to make sure all of Annabeth's things were together.

And now three hours later she stumbled through her kitchen, wiping her swollen eyes and red nose, as saying goodbye to Annabeth and Kendra had gutted her.

Somehow she needed to pull herself together, shower and find the courage to face Jake, who would be done with milking soon. She wanted to catch him before he headed to the fields so she could get on the road as quickly as possible.

Put Holland Hill behind her.

After her second cup of strong coffee and a hot shower, Tori stood in the middle of her bedroom with dove-gray walls and white trim, the restored iron headboard she'd purchased from Agnes James's shop in town, and bed covered in an aqua-and-gray mosaic-patterned comforter. She loved this room. The way Jake had taken her ideas and transformed it into an oasis of light and peace with the sheer curtains, lots of plants and the small indoor fountain waterfall.

She opened the French doors, allowing the morning

sunlight to spill across the refinished hardwood floor as the cool morning air lifted the sheer curtains like a bridal veil.

The scents of the farm wafted from the pasture and curled around her, causing tears to flood her eyes once again. She wouldn't be able to pass a farm without thinking of Jake. Problem was, he wasn't far from her thoughts no matter how much distance was between them.

An hour later, wearing a red dress that gave her more confidence than she felt, Tori dragged two suitcases to her car and hefted them into her trunk.

She closed her trunk and heard a vehicle approaching. Her heart rate picked up speed as she recognized Jake's blue F-150 barreling down the road, kicking up dust.

She wanted to run. To hide. Someplace where she wouldn't have to face him.

But she couldn't do that.

It was time to be brave no matter how much her body trembled.

He parked behind her car and jumped out of his truck, slamming the door.

He pulled off his sunglasses as he strode toward her, his dark brows knitted tightly as lines around his mouth deepened. Still dressed in dirty faded jeans, a tan T-shirt advertising the local feed store, black barn boots and his worn Ohio State ball cap, he still managed to make Tori's pulse quicken.

He stopped in front of her, splayed a hand on his hip and glared at her. "You're leaving. Without saying goodbye."

"No. I mean yes, I'm leaving, but I was going to say goodbye."

"Why?"

"I felt you deserved a goodbye in person this time."

"Why are you leaving?"

"Because, Jake, we just can't seem to connect."

Jake took a step forward, molded his hand around the side of her face and pulled her closer as his mouth covered hers. Then she took a step back as she engraved the memory of his kiss onto her heart.

He scrubbed a hand across the back of his neck and exhaled. "I don't know…seems like we connect very well, Tori. I love you. What more can I say to make you stay?"

She shook her head as tears pooled in her eyes. "It's not enough."

"Tell me what you want and it's yours."

She reached for his hand. "Come with me."

"Tori…" A look of anguish twisted his face. "You know that's impossible."

She swallowed several times and tried to regain her composure. "Then there's nothing more to say." She reached through the open driver's side window and pulled an envelope from her black leather computer bag and handed it to him.

"What's this?"

"The deed to the house and property. It's yours. No strings. If you could give me a couple of weeks to get settled and get my stuff out, I'd appreciate it."

He shoved it back at her. "I don't want it. I want you."

"On your terms. I've spent my life pleasing others only to end up with more baggage than I care to handle. I love you, Jake. I do, with all my heart. But it's not enough. Like I told you yesterday—I need to be someone's priority for a change. I want a home filled with love and laughter and children. I want to belong, Jake, and I won't compromise anymore. With you or anyone else. I'm driving to Pittsburgh to spend a couple of days with Sophie, then I may fly out to California because even though it's been only a couple of hours, I miss Annabeth already." Tori wiped a tear off her cheek, stepped forward and brushed a kiss across Jake's lips, then reached for her door handle.

She started her engine, snapped her seat belt in place, then shifted the car into Reverse and edged around Jake's truck.

As she shifted into Drive, she glanced in her rear-view mirror. Jake stood, frozen in place, and watched her drive away. She headed down Holland Hill, her broken heart scattering across the fields.

She left.

He couldn't believe it. Despite telling her he loved her, Tori got in her car and drove away. His words weren't enough to make her stay.

Jake crushed the envelope Tori had given into a ball, jerked open his driver's side door and tossed it on the seat. He backed out of the driveway, spitting gravel, and raced down the road. He pulled into the barnyard and slammed out of the truck. Cutting hay could wait. He stalked across the road, climbed over the fence and strode through the pasture until he reached the creek.

The canopy of trees sheltered him from the mid-morning sun. Usually the birdsongs settled him, but today he wanted to yell at them to shut up. The flowing water trickled and tumbled over rocks, branches and litter, but it continued moving forward.

Why couldn't he be like that? Why did he feel so stuck? Stagnant?

Kicking over an upturned log, he positioned it so he could sit, then he scooped up a handful of stones.

He hefted them in his hand, then one by one, he whipped them across the water with as much strength as he could manage. His shoulder burned and his hand ached, but he didn't care. The muscles in his arm quivered. His pulse pounded in his ears as his heart rammed against his rib cage, splintering into pieces inside his chest.

"Planning to take down Goliath?"

Jake turned to find his father standing on the bank behind him.

"Aren't you supposed to be on your honeymoon?"

"Soon. Saw you heading for the creek and figured I'd check to make sure everything was okay."

"I'm fine."

"Yeah, you look it. Can't say the same for those bushes across the water. With the way you're whipping those rocks. What's going on?" Dad settled on the log next to him.

"Tori left. She's gone. For good."

"You sure about that?"

"She gave me the deed to the house and property but asked for a couple of weeks to get her things moved. Seemed pretty final to me."

"Did she say why?"

"I told her I love her, but it wasn't enough. I'm not enough for her. I never was." Jake picked up another handful of stones, but instead of throwing them, he shifted them from hand to hand.

"I don't think that's it. I don't think she understands

how to accept love as the gift it is. She feels love needs to be earned."

"Her father did a number on her, but I'm not like him."

"I know you're not. What do you want, Jake?"

"I want my wi— I want Tori."

"Then why are you sitting by the river?"

"She left, Dad."

"Go after her."

He dropped the stones, wiped his hands on his jeans and stood. "I can't."

"Why not?"

"I can't leave the farm." Jake waved a hand across the fields. "There's too much to do, and with the Fatigues to Farming program starting… I can't walk away from that."

Dad raised an eyebrow and shot him a direct look. "Can't or won't?"

"I won't ignore my responsibilities again, Dad."

"What about your responsibility to Tori? To yourself?" Dad pushed to his feet. "You're one of the most responsible men I know, of any age, but the farm is a family business. It's not up to you to carry it on your own. If you choose to leave, go with my blessing. This farm will survive without you, and it will be here when you come back. Don't allow it to take priority over the one you love."

He wished he'd grabbed a rod out of his truck before he headed down to the creek. At least he'd have something to do with his hands other than jamming them in his pockets or throwing stones.

"Tori asked me to go with her and when I said she asked the impossible, she said she needed to be with someone who considered her a priority. I tried to tell her I wanted to have what you and Mom, what Granddad and Grandma had. I wanted to pass down a legacy."

"Son, a legacy isn't a place or a thing. A legacy happens through the people you love and the lives you change. It's rooted in faith and integrity. Find your hope, then work like crazy to hold on to it. There's always hope. Even in the heartache."

"How do you do it, Dad? Keep the faith despite everything you've lost?"

"Faith is believing without seeing. Even when facing adversity, I had two choices—walk by sight or walk by faith. Even when everything around me was falling apart, I chose faith. Because somehow or someway, God always shows up. So it's a choice you make, Jacob—trust God's unfailing goodness or doubt Him and try to get by on your own. I promise you God's way is going to offer you the peace you've been craving for quite some time."

"How do you know that?"

"You've lost your way, son. Take some time and talk to God. See which direction He sends you." Dad touched his shoulder and pulled him into a hug. "I'm going back to the house to take my wife on our honeymoon. Go after Tori, Jake. She's worth it."

As Dad headed back to the house, Jake returned to the log and buried his head in his hands.

God, where do I go from here?

Chapter Fifteen

Jake had nothing left to lose but he had so much more to gain, provided Tori was willing to give him a second chance to make things right.

He pulled up in front of a Tudor-style home on a large corner lot and checked the house number against the address plugged into his phone's GPS. Seeing he was at the right place, Jake reached for a small pink-and-green-striped gift bag on the passenger seat and slipped out of the truck, taking a moment to brush lint off his gray dress pants.

He followed the sidewalk to the covered front porch, where two wicker chairs with yellow cushions sat on each side of the black front door. Taking a deep breath and exhaling slowly, he rang the doorbell.

The door opened, and Sophie, wearing a loose blue shirt with a peacock on the front over black leggings, welcomed him with a smile. "Well, now, if it isn't the hunky country boy. Jake, right?"

"Yes, ma'am."

"Good thing you're so handsome. I'll forgive you for

the ma'am part. Call me Sophie. Come in. I'm going to assume you're here to see Tori."

"Yes, ma—Sophie."

She smiled and waved for him to follow her. "Good. Took you long enough to get here."

"Sometimes it takes a while for common sense to kick in."

"You've got that right." Sophie led him through a room filled with plants and stopped in front of a set of double doors. "Tori's sitting on the lanai. Go and put a smile to her face."

"I'll do my best."

Jake turned the handle and stepped onto the brick-lined covered patio. Manicured privacy bushes at least seven feet high lined three sides of the long, narrow yard. A trickling waterfall cascaded into a small in-ground pond.

Tori sat in the corner at a round metal-and-stone-tile table with her knees pulled up and her back to him. Her ever-present iPad and cell phone sat next to a half-finished glass of iced tea. "Sophie, what do you think about checking out Jeanne's tonight for dinner? Their website offers a gluten-free menu for you."

He shoved his hands in his front pockets and rocked back on his heels. "I'd prefer if you had dinner with me."

Tori whipped around as her hand flew to her mouth. "Jake. What are you doing here?"

"To see you. To talk."

Tori rose to her feet and clasped her hands in front of her. "What do you want to talk about?"

He shrugged. "I don't know…the weather, the latest Pirates game or maybe the fact that you've been gone for a day, and I miss you like crazy."

"Jake—"

He held up a hand. "Let me talk, please."

She nodded and waved a hand to the cushioned patio chair next to hers. "Have a seat. Want some iced tea or lemonade? Sophie may have a soda in the fridge."

Tori brushed past him, but he caught her wrist and tugged her gently to him. "Tori, I'm fine, especially now that I'm here with you." He slid a stray piece of her hair away from her face and tucked it behind her ear. "I missed you."

"I think you said that already."

"I wanted to make sure you really knew it. It was a mistake to let you go."

"I had to leave."

He pressed a finger to her lips. "Shh, my turn to talk. It was a mistake to let you go by yourself."

"What are you saying?"

"I love you, Victoria, and I want to spend the rest of my life showing you how much if you'll let me. You *are* the one I prayed for."

"What about the farm? And the Fatigues to Farming program?"

"The farm's still there. Evan's hanging around to lend a hand, and Dad and Claudia can manage the program."

She placed a hand on his chest. "But you love the farm. Your goal this spring was to get the program started."

He reached for her hand and twined his fingers through hers. "But I love you more. You're my first priority...well, second actually."

"Who's your first?"

"Well, God and I are on good terms again."

"How'd that happen?"

"He showed up."

She smiled, that dimple that set his heart on fire appearing. "Like He always does."

"Dad and I had a talk about what it means to carry on a family legacy. He said a legacy is built on faith and integrity. He also feels I've been trying to offer hope to the disabled veterans as a way of rebuilding hope for myself. It was so tough losing Mom and you and Leo and Micah. So much loss wiped out my hope. Micah accused me of being afraid to take risks. And he was right. I've wrapped myself in a cocoon at the farm, in an environment that I could somewhat control."

"You've been through a lot, and I didn't make it easier for you." She lowered her gaze.

"It's been a trial, but I realized God was with me all along, even when I was angry with Him. Dad also reminded me we have to find the hope in the heartache." Jake reached over and grabbed the gift bag off the table and handed it to Tori. "I brought you something."

She took it, pulled out the tissue paper, and removed a framed photo of the two of them dancing at Dad and Claudia's wedding. She touched the glass and looked up at him with a smile. "It's perfect."

"There's something else in the bottom of the bag."

She peeked inside and pulled out an acorn. She held it up and gave him a puzzled look. "An acorn?"

"From my grandparents' tree at Bridal Bend. They overcame a lot of obstacles to be together and created a legacy of faith and commitment. I want that for us. We can plant that wherever you want, whether it's in Pittsburgh or California. Wherever you go, I'll be with you."

She rolled the acorn between her fingers and looked at the framed photo again. She set them on the table, wrapped her arms around his neck and whispered in his ear, "How about Holland Hill?"

"What about your job? The partnership?"

"Sophie and I did some chatting of our own. She felt with today's technology, I can work from home and return to Pittsburgh a couple of times a month."

"Is that what you want to do? Don't do this because of me."

"I'm doing this because of us. I don't want you to give up the farm. I just wanted to be a priority in your life."

Jake pulled her closer. "And you are. I promise."

"There's just one problem."

"What's that?"

"I don't have a place to live anymore. You have the deed to my house."

"Your home will always be with me, no matter where we end up. Let's plant that tree and grow our legacy together. Marry me, Tori. Again." Jake lowered his head and claimed her lips.

She returned his kiss, then pressed her hand against his chest. "I love you, Jake. And I'd love nothing more than to be your wife. Again."

A peace he hadn't felt in so long settled over him, giving him rest for his soul and offering a hope he'd been too afraid to reach out and grasp. Jake kissed her again, then wrapped Tori in the shelter of his embrace, ready to risk it all to have a second chance at love in this new season of hope.

* * * * *

If you loved this story,
pick up Love Inspired author Lisa Jordan's
previous books set in Shelby Lake

Lakeside Reunion
Lakeside Family
Lakeside Sweethearts
Lakeside Redemption
Lakeside Romance

Available now from Love Inspired!

Find more great reads at
LoveInspired.com

Dear Reader,

Growing up down the road from my grandparents' dairy farm, my favorite memories are filled with feeding calves, the rope swing in the hay barn, large family gatherings, and the values of faith, family and hard work instilled by my grandparents, my mom, aunts and uncles.

In *Season of Hope*, as a former Marine, Jake wants to honor the friend he lost by creating a Fatigues to Farming program, which will allow veterans with disabilities to learn farming in order to start their own small businesses. This idea is based on actual programs around the United States. Farmers are the backbone of America, and our veterans have sacrificed much to protect our freedoms. Both of these noble occupations need to be respected and honored.

When I created this series, I wanted to show how the Holland family uses their faith to find hope in heartache. Faith is believing without seeing, and when we're walking through the valley of darkness, it can be difficult to see the Light, but no matter what challenges we're facing, God is with us every step of the way, waiting to lead us through those difficult seasons. Hold onto the Hope.

I love hearing from my readers, so please email me at lisa@lisajordanbooks.com. Visit my website at lisajordanbooks.com to learn more about upcoming novels and events.

Be blessed,
Lisa Jordan

THE AMISH SPINSTER'S COURTSHIP
by Emma Miller
When Marshall Byler meets Lovey Stutzman—a newcomer to his Amish community—it's love at first sight. Except Lovey doesn't believe the handsome bachelor is serious about pursuing her. And with his grandmother trying to prevent the match, will they ever find their way to each other?

THEIR CONVENIENT AMISH MARRIAGE
Pinecraft Homecomings • by Cheryl Williford
The last thing widowed single mother Verity Schrock expects is to find her former sweetheart back in town—with a baby. Now the bishop and Leviticus Hilty's father are insisting they marry for their children's sake. Can a marriage of convenience cause love to bloom between the pair again?

THE RANCHER'S LEGACY
Red Dog Ranch • by Jessica Keller
Returning home isn't part of Rhett Jarrett's plan—until he inherits the family ranch from his father. Running it won't be easy with his ranch assistant, Macy Howell, challenging all his decisions. But when he discovers the truth about his past, will he begin to see things her way?

ROCKY MOUNTAIN DADDY
Rocky Mountain Haven • by Lois Richer
In charge of a program for foster youths, ranch foreman Gabe Webber is used to children...but fatherhood is completely different. Especially since he just found out he has a six-year-old son. Now, with help from Olivia DeWitt, who's temporarily working at the foster kids' retreat, Gabe must learn how to be a dad.

HER COLORADO COWBOY
Rocky Mountain Heroes • by Mindy Obenhaus
Socialite Lily Davis agrees to take her children riding...despite her fear of horses. Working with widowed cowboy Noah Stephens to launch his new rodeo school is a step further than she planned to go. But they might just discover a love that conquers both their fears.

INSTANT FATHER
by Donna Gartshore
When his orphaned nephew has trouble at school, Paul Belvedere must turn to the boy's teacher, Charlotte Connelly, for assistance. But as the little boy draws them together, can Paul trust Charlotte with his secret...and his heart?

Get 4 FREE REWARDS!

We'll send you 2 FREE Books plus 2 FREE Mystery Gifts.

Love Inspired® books feature contemporary inspirational romances with Christian characters facing the challenges of life and love.

Their Family Legacy — Lorraine Beatty

The Rancher's Answered Prayer — Arlene James

FREE Value Over **$20**

YES! Please send me 2 FREE Love Inspired® Romance novels and my 2 FREE mystery gifts (gifts are worth about $10 retail). After receiving them, if I don't wish to receive any more books, I can return the shipping statement marked "cancel." If I don't cancel, I will receive 6 brand-new novels every month and be billed just $5.24 for the regular-print edition or $5.74 each for the larger-print edition in the U.S., or $5.74 each for the regular-print edition or $6.24 each for the larger-print edition in Canada. That's a savings of at least 13% off the cover price. It's quite a bargain! Shipping and handling is just 50¢ per book in the U.S. and 75¢ per book in Canada.* I understand that accepting the 2 free books and gifts places me under no obligation to buy anything. I can always return a shipment and cancel at any time. The free books and gifts are mine to keep no matter what I decide.

Choose one: ☐ **Love Inspired® Romance Regular-Print** (105/305 IDN GMY4)   ☐ **Love Inspired® Romance Larger-Print** (122/322 IDN GMY4)

Name (please print)

Address   Apt. #

City   State/Province   Zip/Postal Code

Mail to the Reader Service:
IN U.S.A.: P.O. Box 1341, Buffalo, NY 14240-8531
IN CANADA: P.O. Box 603, Fort Erie, Ontario L2A 5X3

Want to try 2 free books from another series? Call 1-800-873-8635 or visit www.ReaderService.com.

---

*Terms and prices subject to change without notice. Prices do not include sales taxes, which will be charged (if applicable) based on your state or country of residence. Canadian residents will be charged applicable taxes. Offer not valid in Quebec. This offer is limited to one order per household. Books received may not be as shown. Not valid for current subscribers to Love Inspired Romance books. All orders subject to approval. Credit or debit balances in a customer's account(s) may be offset by any other outstanding balance owed by or to the customer. Please allow 4 to 6 weeks for delivery. Offer available while quantities last.

Your Privacy—The Reader Service is committed to protecting your privacy. Our Privacy Policy is available online at www.ReaderService.com or upon request from the Reader Service. We make a portion of our mailing list available to reputable third parties that offer products we believe may interest you. If you prefer that we not exchange your name with third parties, or if you wish to clarify or modify your communication preferences, please visit us at www.ReaderService.com/consumerchoice or write to us at Reader Service Preference Service, P.O. Box 9062, Buffalo, NY 14240-9062. Include your complete name and address.

LI19R

They'd both just turned back to their work when a familiar loud, croaking sound cut the silence.

The twins shrieked and ran from where they'd been playing into the little cabin's yard and slammed into Anna, their faces frightened.

"What was that?" Anna sounded alarmed, too, kneeling to hold and comfort both girls.

"Nothing to be afraid of," Sean said, trying to hold back laughter. "It's just egrets. Type of water bird." He located the source of the sound, then went over to the trio, knelt beside them, and pointed through the trees and growth.

When the girls saw the stately white birds, they gasped.

"They're so pretty!" Anna said.

"Pretty?" Sean chuckled. "Nobody from around here would get excited about an egret, nor think it's especially pretty." But as he watched another one land beside the first, white wings spread wide as it skidded into the shallow water, he realized that there was beauty there. He just hadn't noticed it before.

That was what kids did for you: made you see the world through their fresh, innocent eyes. A fist of longing clutched inside his chest.

The twins were tugging at Anna's shirt now, trying to get her to take them over toward the birds. "You may go look as long as you can see me," she said, "but take careful steps by the water." She took the bolder twin's face in her hands. "The water's not deep, but I still don't want you to wade in. Do you understand?"

Both little girls nodded vigorously.

They ran off and she watched for a few seconds, then turned back to her work with a barely audible sigh.

"Go take a look with them," he urged her. "It's not every day kids see an egret for the first time."

"You're sure?"

"Go on." He watched her run like a kid over to her girls. And then he couldn't resist walking a few steps closer and watching them, shielded by the trees and brush.

The twins were so excited that they weren't remembering to be quiet. "It caught a *fish*!" the one was crowing, pointing at the bird, which, indeed, held a squirming fish in its mouth.

"That one's neck is like an S!" The quieter twin squatted down, rapt.

Anna eased down onto the sandy beach, obviously unworried about her or the girls getting wet or dirty, laughing and talking to them and sharing their excitement.

The sight of it gave him a melancholy twinge. His own mom had been a nature lover. She'd taken him and his brothers fishing, visited a nature reserve a few times, back in Alabama where they'd lived before coming here.

Oh, if things were different, he'd run with this, see where it led…

Don't miss
Lee Tobin McClain's Low Country Hero*,*
available March 2019 from HQN Books!

www.Harlequin.com

Looking for inspiration in tales
of hope, faith and heartfelt romance?

Check out **Love Inspired**® and
Love Inspired® **Suspense** books!

New books available every month!

CONNECT WITH US AT:

Facebook.com/groups/HarlequinConnection

 Facebook.com/HarlequinBooks

 Twitter.com/HarlequinBooks

 Instagram.com/HarlequinBooks

 Pinterest.com/HarlequinBooks

ReaderService.com

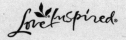

LIGENRE2018R2

Love Inspired®

Inspirational Romance to Warm Your Heart and Soul

Join our social communities to connect with other readers who share your love!

Sign up for the Love Inspired newsletter at **www.LoveInspired.com** to be the first to find out about upcoming titles, special promotions and exclusive content.

CONNECT WITH US AT:

Facebook.com/groups/HarlequinConnection

 Facebook.com/LoveInspiredBooks

 Twitter.com/LoveInspiredBks

LISOCIAL2018